FIT THE CRIME

The Impenetrable Lie

BOOK 6

CORINNE ARROWOOD

TABLE OF CONTENTS

A Special Note

The statistics of PTSD are staggering. Many of our Marines and soldiers come home entrenched in the horrors they experienced and the nightmares they cannot escape. If you know one of our heroes that might be suffering from PTSD, contact Wounded Warrior Project, National Center for PTSD, VA Caregiver Support Line at 888-823-7458.

The Impenetrable Lie

WHAT ABOUT REG

*T*rinity and Babe were more than ready to hear Reg's story. It was something that had perplexed them. His first explanation was his dad was in the service and died; another time, he said his parents were dopers; neither tale rang true. He chose the best parts of Chris' and Jacob's stories, but there was no authenticity. He was different than the other two boys.

Babe stood watch over her. "Girl, sit on the chariot seat and take the ride down. No stairs until you build more strength in your legs." With a dejected look on her face, she boarded the lift chair. Once it came to a stop, she wanted to get up; he could see it in her eyes, but she was hesitant. He stood in front of her. She pushed up. Her legs shook from the stress she put on her muscles. "Sit. Don't rush. Oxygenate your blood. Take some deep breaths, and if you need to use the wheelchair, do so. You're going to have to build endurance. I know you are excited, but chillax, okay?" He kissed the top of her head.

Inside his body, Babe was rejoicing with almost nervous jitters. Her walking and maneuvering was the moment they'd hoped and dreamed about. He contrasted the beautiful yet lifeless form that occupied a hospital bed for months. Never admitting it aloud, he feared life as he knew it was over. The doctors might as well cut him open and remove his heart because he'd never have their perfect life again. He and the God entity had many conversations in the middle of the night when sleep was unattainable. The faint voice always referenced Job from the Bible. Yes, what Job went through was horrifying, but they were words on a page to him. *Say what?*

Trinity would have fussed; it made him smile. What, so someone had it worse than him? He got the message and was thankful she was alive. Trinity had come a long way, far surpassing any expectations. His lady was one feisty, determined soul.

Irritated with a near scowl, she complained, "Shit, I want everyone to see me walk, don't you get it? I want to show my mom and dad especially. They have no faith in me. Shame on them." With a hint of pent-up anger, she stood and grabbed the wheelchair, using it to steady herself like pushing a grocery cart. "There's more than one way to skin a cat." She grinned, and Reg smiled at her sassiness. The three of them went into the family room, plopping on the sofa.

"Reg, I normally wouldn't allow it, but you're opening up a huge scar that could be painful. Want a shot of whiskey?" The boy shrugged. "Try it; maybe it will calm your nerves, maybe not. You don't need to be nervous. You are family and can tell us anything." Babe poured two drams of Glenlivet, handing one to the sixteen-year-old. An endless stream of possibilities flew through his mind. Perhaps he was the one who needed the dram most of all. Reg appeared in control.

The boy put the glass to his mouth and took a tiny sip. "Do I have to drink this? You drink this shit? It's worse than pizza vomit. That's nasty and burns the piss out of my mouth."

Babe smiled, "A few more sips will numb your mouth. Talk."

"I'm scared to tell y'all. I don't want to leave here, and you might make me if I talk."

Babe leaned into their conversation, "Dig deep and find your courage. I have no intention of sending you away. Start, no more dodging the subject." The big guy stared directly into Reg's eyes. Trinity stroked his arm and nodded. The boy started to turn his head; Babe stopped him with a finger and turned so they were face to face.

Reg began his story. "You might get pissed." He looked down into his hands, stalling. "My mom and dad are Elizabeth and David Eglin. We live, or they live, in Baton Rouge. My dad is a medical salesperson. He does well. I have a little sister; she is five years younger than me. I thought we were a happy, everyday kind of family." His head dropped to his chest, and the tears began.

"Don't be ashamed of your tears. Let them flow; it's good not to hold them inside. And?" Babe asked. He watched the boy's micro-expressions. The pain was beginning to be more than the teen could handle. "Take another sip, or just throw it down your throat in one big gulp," he smiled. "Reg, it's all going to be okay. You trust me?" The boy nodded. "Almost everything has an explanation. Almost." Babe remembered back to when he was a child, and what was the reasonable explanation for the abuse his father unleashed on him? There was nothing explainable or okay about it.

Reg swigged the dram down, causing him to wrinkle his forehead and nose. His lips turned downward as he stuck his tongue out and coughed. "That's disgusting. You don't lie, sir; my mouth is numb like novocaine. You warned me it would numb me up, like the dentist." Babe had always noticed that Reg had more social graces, and somewhere in his past, he knew how to charm and admire the finer things in life. Someone had loved and guided him. The other two boys had probably never seen a dentist. "Mom and Dad took us, me and my little sister, Ellie, to New Orleans to the Aquarium. I was excited. I could have stayed there for hours. Then, I spotted the gift shop; I wanted a stupid rubber shark. My dad said he'd buy a tee shirt but didn't want to buy the trinket trash. I acted like a brat. Ellie started whining, and Dad told Mom he'd get the car and that the three of us could wait outside. I wanted to look at the sharks again. I was a pretty responsible kid; even though I was only ten, I told her I'd stand next to another family or the Aquarium personnel in the area. Mom said okay, and she picked up Ellie to catch up with Dad. Given the downtown traffic, they instructed me to be on the lookout for them; they'd be about fifteen or twenty minutes. I checked my watch and hauled ass to the shark tank. Some of the deadly creatures were massive. Then, this lady in a black dive suit got in with them, and I thought, "That's what I wanted to be when I grew up. It was so badass." He continued that he had checked his watch, and it had been thirty minutes, so he ran to the entrance and waited. He said he waited and waited, but his parents never came back. He started to cry, saying he shouldn't have complained about the rubber shark.

The effects of the dram of Glenlivet started to take effect, and he became less inhibited. Babe put his arm around him, giving him a squeeze. "So you waited for how long?"

"Until the night security guy said he would call the police. I ran as fast as I could. A group of kids was smoking cigarettes and hanging out by Café du Monde. They were cool and, from the start, accepted me as part of the group. They taught me a lot about survival, picking pockets, and making friends with some shop and restaurant managers. They couldn't believe my parents left me. I have nightmares about waiting outside of The Aquarium, and the fear strikes like it did when they left me. Sometimes, I twist my dreams and have them pull up in the car, but I can't get in for some reason. So, Sir, you wanted my story, and that's it. They left me at the Aquarium, and I haven't been back." The boy's shoulders shuddered as he fought against emotions.

Babe figured there had to be more to it than that. Trinity held Reg's hand while the big guy grilled about the month, the make of the vehicle, and where they had parked. Reg could answer most of the questions but had no idea where they had parked; he was too excited about the thought of going to the Aquarium to pay attention. Babe mentally noted the parents' names, car, and month. It was before school ended, but after Easter, probably April or May 2018, he had a last name. Until then, Reg claimed his surname as Jackson, Reggie Jackson. *Kids!*

They had enough information to research and find his parents. It didn't add up. There was more to the story. From his description of his family, they seemed to be an average upper-middle-class family. No matter the status, there were always a few skeletons in the closet, but that was a fact of being human.

"Y'all, thank you for listening. I'm sure my mom and dad had their reasons, and it wasn't the dang rubber shark. Don't be hatin' on them."

There was pleading in his voice; he sat up straight, shoulders back as though he was ready to take on the world.

Babe stood, turned, and questioned, "Be hatin'? Is that what private education is teaching you?" The big man chuckled as the boy started for the stairs. "Reg, I am not in a position to judge anyone. Where are Chris and Jake? Your dad's name is David?"

The boy started up the stairs and called out in a loud whisper, "Chris is on the phone, and Jake is playing one of his games. David Reginald Eglin." Then, all went quiet upstairs.

Babe sat in the study at his computer and looked up David Reginald Eglin. Trinity went into the kitchen and heard Ruthie talking to the baby. She had set up the pack n' play in the kitchen and spoke to Chancée about cooking. "I tried not to listen in on y'all's conversation, but I couldn't help but hear a few things. There is a piece missing to that puzzle if you ask me, and ma'am, I believe you owe the money jar."

He found numerous articles about the man. Reg's dad owned a medical equipment company in Baton Rouge along with his sister, Elloise Dupont. They did exceptionally well. From all accounts, the man was a good guy, philanthropic, and a pillar in the community. Reg looked like a kid version of the man. It didn't fit that he would abandon his ten-year-old son.

After the fourth article, he hit pay-dirt with a brief death notice, clearing up any confusion. It would be painful for the kid to hear, but he could have solace knowing they hadn't abandoned him. To be frank, Babe found it particularly disturbing that the aunt didn't look for the boy. It was something Gino would have done—take the money and run.

David Reginald Eglin and his wife, Elizabeth Goldman Eglin of Baton Rouge, Louisiana, along with daughter Elloise Elizabeth Eglin, aged 5, died on Saturday, May 19th, 2018, in a fatal automobile accident in New Orleans. They are survived by Mr. Eglin's sister, Elloise Eglin Dupont, widow of Steven

Ambrose Dupont of Baton Rouge, Louisiana. David Eglin is predeceased by his mother, Jaqueline Butler Eglin, and father, Reginald David Eglin. Sydney and Virginia Goldman predeceased their daughter, Elizabeth Goldman Eglin. Private service by invitation only.

Why is there no mention of Reg? Babe scribbled info about the sister, and he would chase it up. His senses tingled, and he couldn't help but think Reg's aunt capitalized on the death of her brother. Babe, as Reg's legal guardian, would look unsavory about acting in the role of his attorney as well, but Mays Connolly certainly could, or one of his partners.

The boy had been so good with Chancée, and now it made sense. What sixteen-year-old boy wants to be troubled with a baby? With Trinity's prodding, Babe pondered if Reg would remember his aunt. She obviously knew there had been two children, yet she hadn't put it in the paper. *Strange.* Reg would have his father's share of the business in his own right. How many others knew of Reg, and why hadn't anyone spoken up?

Babe needed to do more research. There were multiple things to consider: the sale of the Eglin's house, any investments, life insurance, and any other property his parents may have owned. Who had power of attorney for his parents regarding their Wills? There were many pieces to a puzzle that needed explanation.

One Sunday looked like any other Sunday at the Noelle's. The entire family met at St. Dominic's for Mass, then headed to the Noelle's home for Sunday dinner and hanging with their cousins. Babe no longer held a grudge outwardly against Trinity's parents, not that anyone would have known; he was just a little quieter and smiled less. He kept it well under wraps. From conversations, only Bethany and her parents were privy to the Angelette duplicity, at least from the Noelle side of the family.

Babe kept an eye on Trinity, waiting for her to demonstrate that she could walk. She moved her foot on and off the footrest several times.

While Babe was cordial, his relationship with those in the conspiracy suffered a few dents. Betrayal, lies, and dishonesty were at the top of Babe's most despicable list. Broken trust was nearly impossible to rectify. Trinity rolled to him. "Boy, you look mighty thoughtful. What's running through your mind?" Her smile sent a warm flush through his body. His pulse raced anytime he was in close proximity to his spicey lady. Memories of her untimely comment as they entered St. Dominic for Mass echoed in his head. 'Hey Vic, when I'm in the chair, it is the perfect height to unzip' and how he shut that shit down with a look of disbelief at her unabashed inappropriateness. He glanced around to ensure no one else heard her. He felt the tips of his ears turning crimson. *Divert conversation.*

"Wondering when you are going to break in the element of surprise. I want to make sure I am there to watch people's expressions." He smiled down at her. She was nothing short of amazing. She may never dance on Louie's bartop again, but, by God, she would dance again somewhere, and he would dance with her, awkward or not. "You are thoughtful, more than usual today. What's wrong? Babe, your ears are pink. Are you thinking naughty thoughts?" She double-raised her brows. He shook his head and said there was no point in talking about it. In all truth, he felt even more out of place with little purpose. She could walk now and was mending at a rate of speed, impressing the doctors.

Watching the interaction with the family, he wondered if they'd ever pulled such a breach with anyone else. No matter how much they had included him in things, there was always the feeling that he wasn't one of them. He felt settled in his house uptown with Trinity, the boys, and the princess; he belonged; they were his people. It was his domain; he was mere surplus to requirements at the Noelle's. Trinity pushed again. "You won't understand, ma girl. You fit in anywhere, and this isn't me being some sad sack. It's been the story of my life. I felt more comfortable before the charade, but I was never one of the boys. I like your brothers; I do. Maybe independently is the best description." He blew out a deep breath.

"Then there's Reg. That's going to be a tough talk, telling the kid his parents died, and that's why they didn't come for him. There are a couple of unknowns. Will he feel better that they hadn't abandoned him, or will he feel guilty about not wanting to leave and making them come pick him up? See? And then what of the aunt? Something smells rotten in Denmark, as they say." She nodded and understood. She kissed the top of his hand. There was no need to go into life without purpose; she'd never understand that concept.

A book of unspoken thoughts loomed in everything—in their private talks, dinner round the table bantering, even in their bed. The tragedy had not only come close to taking Trinity's life, but it stole or put a damper in all areas of their lives. He felt like it was a spirit of doom, maybe even a nagging evil spawn. *C'mon God. Give us a break. Don't let the ruse come between Trinity and me.*

Antoine interrupted his contemplative moment while his woman continued with constant chatter and hypotheses, creating a background from which to think. "Baby girl, I hope you don't mind me barging in on your conversation." He held her hand. "I wanted to tell your Marine that I had nothing over his head and that if re-joining was what he wanted, then so be it." Looking at Trinity, he explained, "I had made it known to your husband that I didn't want him far from home, such as re-enlisting."

She patted his hand. "Oh, Daddy, have no fear. Babe plays by his own rules, and no one has a ring in his nose that leads him around. Nope, my man is an entity unto himself." Babe's eyes volleyed from Trinity to her dad back and forth. Antoine clearly pulled every card he had to win favor with Babe. *What the fuck difference does it matter if he approves or not. That song has played, and the dance is over.* "And, Daddy, I have a trick up my sleeve." She stood. The silence was punctuated by her mother invading it with squeals of thanks be to God. "How ya like them apples?"

The excitement in the room was electric. Babe leaned down and told her not to push it. Trinity walked a few steps and then walked back to the wheelchair, grabbed the handles, and moved it to the buffet line. Everyone hugged her. Antoinette was full of tears, and Antoine actually had a look of glee with a full-blown smile, which was a novelty. Since meeting Antoine, Babe felt everything the man did was for the family, but the manipulation with Angelette was far more sinister. The excuse of keeping the baby from him was just that, an excuse. What was the real reason? Control over him? *That ain't gonna happen.* He didn't like the games her family played. While the military wasn't everyone's cup of tea, things would be entirely different if the U.S. did like Israel and made it mandatory that everyone, men and women alike, served for two years and eight months and could be drafted until age forty. Perhaps there wouldn't be as much dishonesty, greed, or games. None of those things would last a second when each life depended on the life next to them; like it or not, some aspects of the military would parlay into a much healthier society—not so me, me, me, and entitled.

"How long have y'all known Trinity could walk?" Bethany's voice was sweet and quiet. How could someone so genteel devise such a scandalous and deceptive scheme? She set the stage for her sister's husband to sleep with another woman. Babe knew he was guilty, but he told Trinity about it, which didn't make it right, but it was some kind of statement. What about Carmen? How could he so easily dismiss that? Why hurt Trinity any more than he had? It would serve no purpose. The God entity knew, and he'd have to answer one day for it, especially since it was one of the big ten. Thoughts for another day? First, he had to get through the Sunday Noelle bullshit. "Babe, are you angry with me? I didn't mean to hurt anyone." Bethany steepled her hands as though in prayer, almost begging without words.

He stood still for a moment, then looked down at her. "No, Bethany, I'm not angry with you; I'm disappointed that you would betray your sister in such a way. I'm nothing, my feelings don't matter, but your sister? That is a whole different can of worms. The day will come when she will address it and probably kick Angelette's ass. She loves you, no matter what." Her jaw dropped. That was the most the man had ever said to her at one time, and it cut straight into her heart. Bethany's eyes filled with tears. She was truly regretful, but it still didn't excuse anything for Babe. It was betrayal, plain and simple, and yes, he was guilty, he knew, maybe not the first or second time, but after that, he knew and did it anyway. *Move on, Marine*, he pushed. He put his arm around her shoulder. "Truce?"

As a tear trickled down her cheek, she whispered, "Truce." She rose on her tiptoes and pulled his head down so she could kiss his cheek. The questions about when Trinity knew she could walk and when he knew she could walk bombarded them. He admitted he'd known it for weeks but also knew she had to come to the decision herself, so he didn't push too hard.

Emotions are a funny thing, he thought; they could switch in a heartbeat. He was angry to the point of nausea with Bethany, but her woeful, teary eyes switched the emotion to forgiveness and family love. Maybe things might straighten up one day, there was no doubt. It was all about time and circumstance. He guarded Trinity closely with watchful eyes. She had forgiven all, maybe not Angelette, but those feelings were more of a primal nature. The girl had tried to claim Trinity's man as hers by seducing him to bed. Trinity and Babe hadn't had enough bedtime to erase the damage done by Angelette.

Trinity slowly walked up to Babe, "I'm exhausted. Can we go home?" The boys wanted to stay longer, and a couple of the uncles said they'd drive them home. *Nope.* "We'll Uber home, and Chris can take them later." She called Chris to her. "Be careful; it's a bigger car than you are used to." Babe took Chancée's seat out of the new kidmobile so they could Uber home with the baby. Babe bought the Expedition as a welcome home for Trinity; besides, the family needed more room. While she couldn't drive yet, it was only a matter of time before she'd be ratting the streets.

When they arrived at the house via Uber, Clive was dropping off Ruthie. "Yo Babe," Clive hollered. The men did the one-armed hug thing. He saw

Trinity take a few steps. "Wow, Miss Trinity, you are recovering well." She smiled, but her eyes looked tired.

"I'm putting this one to bed, but if you want to watch a game or play some one-on-one, I'll go for it. You'll spank the shit out of me, but that's okay."

WHAT'S IN A NAME

The morning sun peeked through the curtains. Babe had already finished his workout and run. After getting out of the shower, he heard the princess squirming. Before the ear-piercing call of the wild, he hurriedly made it to the crib. "Shh, Mommy's sleeping."

In a low rumbly drone, Trinity spoke, "No, she's not." He lay the baby in their bed and got dressed. "Where are you going? Wait, let me guess. You are going to Baton Rouge to Reg's dad's company and then find the aunt. Boy, I'd like to be a fly on that wall."

"Come with me." He zipped up his jeans, buckled his belt, and put his boots on. "Take your time getting together; I still have to research addresses and talk with Mays. I hope he handles all the legal mumbo jumbo." She cuddled with Chancée, barely hearing anything Babe was saying.

"Babe, you said you thought things were rotten in Denmark. How about Norway?"

He smiled and said things were perfect in Norway, and anytime she wanted to go, to say the word. With sass in her voice, she told him to hurry up and figure out the Reg family issue because she was ready to travel.

After Babe had an hour on the computer and a half hour on the phone with Mays, Trinity managed to feed the baby and herself, fold a load of clothes, and walk around the first floor as though there had never been a life-threatening attack and almost a year of recovery. She took his advice and didn't try the stairs, figuring she'd fall and the 'return to normal' would be pushed back another year.

With a stack of papers in his hand, he told Trinity to get ready, then stashed some in a chest of drawers in the formal living room. They'd be leaving soon, and he'd fill her in on the way to Baton Rouge.

The drive to Baton Rouge was heavy with traffic, giving Babe plenty of time to unpack the horrible deeds of the aunt. Thus, the story began, Babe explained based on his presumptions and gathered information. Elizabeth got pregnant with Reg while she and David were at L.S.U. It wasn't ideal, but they did the proper thing and married. The aunt was engaged. All formalities were underway when Elizabeth came up expecting, drawing attention to a quick wedding and stealing the spotlight from Elloise. The parents had a wedding announcement in the society section of a Baton Rouge paper announcing Elloise's engagement, but then the celebration and hoopla went silent. The following article was about Elizabeth and David's wedding. Babe was interjecting his opinion about stealing attention, but it aligned perfectly with the research and information he found. The aunt was a real piece of work.

Reg's father, David, ran the company under his father, Reginald Eglin. They named the baby boy after David's dad. Elloise was expected to do the social scene and had ownership in name only, never to actually work at the company. She and her husband didn't want children, so as a familial gesture, David and Elizabeth named their second child, a daughter, after Elloise. Following closely after the birth of their second child, David's parents died in a house fire. They were wealthy and lived in the most prestigious area. Undoubtedly, they would have had a top-notch fire alarm, which not only raised questions in Babe's mind but the fire investigator, at the time, had suspected arson. After a few years of marriage, the aunt's husband died at the hands of a hit-and-run driver. That in itself set off Babe's bullshit-o-meter. It was strange to him that both her husband and brother died in a vehicular accident, and the deaths of her parents by house fire were a stretch as well. Anyone closely involved with the aunt appeared to have an untimely, impractical death. Sure, there were unfortunate house fires and nasty hit-and-run accidents, but for a family to have such a rash of fatalities all leading to a great fortune left to the only living relative was suspect.

Babe had Mays delve into the assets of Reg's parents. It bugged the hell out of him that no one looked for the boy. There had not been one mention or inquiry made, according to Mays, regarding a male child born to David and Elizabeth. Austin Guilbault was the lawyer who handled all of the sister's financial and legal affairs. Mays was a master at research and was determined to find out everything about Mr. Guilbault; no stone was left unturned.

Many articles and press releases showed Austin and Elloise attending the same functions. According to the paper, the attorney was married with three children yet appeared closer than friends with Elloise. Mays called Babe and rattled off the information with addresses and phone numbers. The way the dominoes lined up had to be more than coincidence. Proving intention was always a tricky deal.

Babe got off the interstate and, after winding through a weave of streets, pulled up to an ordinary-looking, no-thrills place called Poor Boy Lloyds. He glanced at Trinity when she started asking questions. "You'll see. This place has the best poboys and brunch specials. It even rivals your Domilises, Mother's, and Louie's," he chuckled. "Seriously, food is excellent, but more than that, we have to map out our course to nail this woman. Maybe the attorney doesn't know he's waiting in line for the death train, or was he a part of the scheme?"

Mays suggested they let him make a call first, as he was the boy's attorney. He would request a meeting since Guilbault was the attorney of record regarding the late David Eglin's estate. Mays found the dad's Will, but it did not mention young Reg; however, the filing date stamp was smudged, so he would need to acquire a true copy. What a shock it would be to hear that the boy was alive. Babe had to find out what Reg remembered of his aunt. The trip to Baton Rouge was premature, and

Babe knew it but was chomping at the bit to get justice for Reg. They could make use of the time driving by the addresses and perhaps pop into Eglin Medical Support. Trinity in the wheelchair would be a perfect set piece. They knew the company distributed to medical supply storefronts, hospitals, and medical offices. The main office was corporate headquarters, not retail. A person of less intelligence passing by might not know, which would appear to be an innocent mistake, and they could feign ignorance.

Mays smiled when a bright, cheery voice answered the phone, "Delery, Guilbault, and Shane, how may I help you?"

"This is Mays Connolly from Atlanta, Georgia." His authentic Southern accent was pleasing to the ear, almost melodic. "I would like to set an appointment with Mr. Austin Guilbault. Can you help with that, or should I speak with his secretary?"

She said she'd patch him through to Ms. Carney, Mr. Guilbault's personal assistant. With a couple of buzzes, a voice answered vastly different than the friendly receptionist. "Office of Austin Guilbault, this is Ms. Carney, his personal assistant. I can set the appointment for you, but I have a few questions." Mays thought her tone was anything but pleasant. "What is it that you wish to speak with him about?"

"Pardon me, ma'am, but I believe that is privileged information. The nature of the visit is to discuss a Last Will and Testament, and I'm afraid that is all the information I can provide. I'm certain you understand." Whether she understood or not was a moot point—either she could schedule the appointment or she wouldn't; there were always other ways to get what he wanted.

With an elongated exhalation edging on curt, she responded, "He has a four o'clock on Tuesday, June 4th." Being May 20th, Mays graciously accepted the appointment, thinking a couple of weeks wasn't too far off. "Unless you could be here tomorrow at nine; he had a cancellation." Her offer bordered on snarky, and he felt assured that the receptionist had said he was from Atlanta.

"Thank you, ma'am, I'll see you tomorrow morning." From the sound of the hmph, it was easy to identify her disappointing surprise.

The following questions that Mays had pertained to how Babe became the boy's legal guardian. Did he go through the proper channels? He called Babe's cell, "I have a question for you, baby brother. Do you have papers proving you are the boy's guardian?"

Babe said their grandfather's attorney and financial advisor had everything drawn up, and yes, it was all by the book. The three boys were indigent, and now they were his. Babe's heart raced, his pulse bound, and sweat poured out of him when he heard the meeting with Guilbault was for the following morning. Mays booked a flight to NOLA, arriving at 7:45 that evening, and he expected they would save him a plate from dinner. The pace was picking up, and soon they would have answers.

They pulled up to the first address. Babe walked by Trinity's side as she rolled into the business. It was a sizeable building with sleek modern lines and plenty of plate glass floor to ceiling, something one might expect in New York or L.A., not Baton Rouge. A security guard greeted them. "Can I help you, folks?"

Trinity responded, "Yes, I was looking for a hammock or sling to move from the bed—"

The man cut her off. "Sorry, Miss. You are at the corporate office, not a storefront, but—"

The elevator dinged as a flashy forty-something emerged with her minions. The security guard smiled at her. "Good Morning," he checked his watch; yes, it was still morning, although it was inching to afternoon. From the condescending and ruthless look on her face, she had no intention of acknowledging the greeting. He looked at Babe and said as though it would impress Babe or Trinity, "Elloise Eglin," and raised his brows. To Babe, she looked like the kind of person that wouldn't give a hearty shit about hiring an assassin— cold and calculating and totally self-absorbed. The number of deaths all linked to each other had neon arrows flashing her way. The tingles spread throughout Babe's body. *What a bitch.*

Trinity could talk to a light post or the President of the U.S. and not bat an eye; one person was the same as the next. She quickly rolled over to the gaggle of wannabes and ass-kissers. "Mrs. Eglin, I'm Trinity Noelle from New Orleans. I read your company makes the best medical equipment. It is such a pleasure to meet you. Y'all do such good work for the physically challenged."

The woman was taken aback at Trinity's boldness and began to sputter but adjusted to posh and sophistication in a snap, not even glancing in Babe's direction. "My, this is not a storefront, dear," she spoke condescendingly. "Order from our catalog, or we have a retailer only 5 minutes away; security can give you the address." She lifted her head high and left with a primadonna attitude.

Following the brief interaction, Trinity rolled over to the security guard, who sported a name tag displaying Wilson. "Mr. Wilson, can you provide us with a catalog and address of the nearest retailer? I take it, Mrs. Eglin," he corrected her and said the lady was not married; Eglin was her maiden name. "Ms. Eglin," Trinity corrected, "seems like an angel to have this company. It helps so many." Babe wondered if Trinity knew how thick she was putting it on, but Wilson soaked up the attention and being in the know.

He returned to his desk, a metallic semi-circle made of side-by-side pipes—*quite cosmo,* Trinity thought. Chatty Wilson provided her with an abundance of information—a magazine about the history of the company, its founders, and a catalog in which he scribbled the address of the nearest retailer. He made an off-the-cuff sarcastic comment about his boss' angelic nature under his breath, but it was loud enough that Trinity heard. She thanked him, and she and Babe returned to their vehicle. "Ma girl, you are

the ballsiest bullshitter I know, but we got a lot of information to digest."
He scooped her out of the wheelchair and placed her in the truck. They
stopped at a convenience store and bought a couple of Baton Rouge society
magazines and newspapers. *Maybe Mzz Eglin might be shown at a society
function,* Babe thought. *More research on the Mzz— maybe penetrate her
inner circle.*

Babe rang Mays, "Bro, I'm heading out of B.R. with my sweet thing. I
got a peek at Mzz Eglin; she seems like a cold bitch. Elloise looks like the
type to kill her parents, husband, and brother. What I still don't get is why
she hadn't mentioned Reg; maybe she thought he died on the streets; I
mean, silver spoon to grunge kid. Truthfully, I never validated any of his
information. It's not like he had a birth certificate or social security card
on him. Both Reg and Jake made up last names. Hell, the boy is entitled
to his pop's social security. If she has been cashing in those checks, that's
punishable by law, and we will press charges."

Mays heard the intensity in Babe's voice. At first, he was just speaking
facts, but the further his diatribe went, the more agitated he became. Odds
were the red radiated up his neck, and if he could get his hands on the
woman—enough thinking. Trinity watched him as the brothers spoke.
"Calm down, Babe, you look insane." One thing was evident: once he
cracked the cocoon of emotion, a flood poured out from all the years of
stuffing them away. Trinity spoke into the phone. "Mays, he'll see you at the
airport tonight. He's getting out of control." The brothers ended the call.
"Get me home, please. Had you not pushed the boy, life would have gone
along just fine. Now, we got this big fucking mess. Have you considered
what you're going to tell Reg?" She poignantly asked.

He snapped back. "It was the right thing to do, and you know it."

In a degrading tone, Elloise demanded, "Wilson, who were those people, and what did they want?" He told her they were simple folks who wanted to buy a hammock. She broke in before he could finish, "Does this look like a store to you? No, unless they are complete morons." She and her entourage headed to the bank of elevators and were gone.

Elloise was a demanding, bullying person. Her only attribute was owning the company. None of the employees were loyal to her, and the talk behind her back was never complimentary. She came across as a spoiled, black-hearted bitch.

She shouted to her assistant to get Austin on the phone. Moments later, her assistant said he was unavailable and would call her later. "Maybe I won't be available!" There was nothing else to do, so she went on an internet shopping spree. "Retail therapy from Neimans always makes me feel better," she whined.

When they reached home, Trinity told Babe to release some of his anger on the heavyweight bag. He had enough time to take twenty minutes on the bag.

Ruthie was in the kitchen with the baby. Trinity parked her wheelchair by the stair lift and walked back to the kitchen. "Ruthie, just when I think we might have a normal everyday kind of life, some sort of crap pops up and stirs the pot." She leaned against the counter and pushed herself up. The tears began to well in her eyes as her breath hitched. "Now that he knows or thinks he knows what happened, it's as though he's on a mission and will make sure the beast of a woman goes to jail, or who knows? He's not one to hit a woman, but you shoulda seen him."

The older woman listened, biting her lip. She waited until there was a natural pause. Ruthie expounded that Trinity knew the kind of man she was married to and how much he loved the boys. She said she'd seen him possibly angrier than Trinity, referring to the beating the girl had by the Amazonian woman. She poured a touch of bourbon into a glass and handed it to the little lady. "Get them tears all gone before he comes in. Maybe good sense will prevail, and Mays will talk some sense into him. He sure don't need to open another can of worms; we got enough worms around here to feed a pond full of fish. We gotta get Chris all ready for graduation and then off to L.S.U. Don't worry, I'll remind him gently about the here and now."

They heard the back door open as Babe came in. He announced he was showering and getting dressed to pick up Mays. Trinity walked him to the stairs and told him to carry her up. She sat on the bed and watched as he removed the stinky, sweaty workout clothes, started the shower, poked his head around the door frame, and asked if he should expect company. With a sly grin, Trinity entered the bathroom void of clothes and joined him in the shower. As the hot water beat down, he apologized for the insanity, saying he'd back away unless Mays' conversation stoked the fire and the aunt sought retribution. As far as Reg was concerned, he planned to talk to him and explain what had happened with his parents and how they'd not abandoned him. If Reg pushed the subject further, they'd cross that bridge when they got to it. Then he let go of the bomb and told her he planned on legally adopting the boys if they wanted; life would be a hell of a lot easier. It was time to head to the airport.

Babe walked around the front of the truck, keeping his eyes on Trinity and beaming with his crooked smile. As soon as he opened the door, he said, "I know I freak you the fuck out. I'm going to step back and let Mays handle everything unless threats are made. Do you understand and concur?"

She put her fingers to her lips and touched his, saying, "I'd expect nothing less."

A FIGHT YOU WON'T WIN

*M*ays came out of the airport with his hanging bag over his shoulder and valise in hand. He looked good. While his face was still roundish, his high cheekbones were more prominent. Trinity hadn't realized how handsome he was before. He had been Mr. Happy Go Lucky, with his pudgy Santa middle, but now he was studly, and the two brothers, while different, made a head-turning pair of bookends. She watched as several women walking into the airport gave him the twice-over.

He slid into the back seat. "Bro, you look like you've been hitting the gym. How's your flight? Anything new in Mays' world?" Babe glanced into the rearview mirror and detected a coy smile on his brother's face. "Spit it out."

Mays hemmed and hawed, then proudly said, "I have a lady friend. You'd approve. Her name is Lark Wells. She's five foot nothing, a little more weight than Trinity, but still thin, and she's my next-door neighbor—blonde, blue-eyed, and personality plus. I got the approval from Mom and Dad. They think she's special. She's a Texas girl, and her Pops is in the oil business, so she's not looking for a money man. The kids like her; shit, she's a kid, 26, a budding young attorney." He handed Trinity his phone. Babe darted a look and expressed his approval. The girl was cute, not drop-dead gorgeous, but she had a great smile and starburst twinkles in her eyes. "And she's looking forward to Norway."

They talked about a Norwegian holiday the rest of the way home. Trinity asked if she had children; the answer was no, but she wanted a couple. The thought of Chancée having cousins close to her age from Babe's family was exciting.

The boys barrelled down the stairs to see Mays. Ruthie set the table for the adults as the boys had already eaten. Babe and Mays discussed the impending conversation with Reg in muffled voices. The plan was for Babe to call Reg to the living room one-on-one. The worry was mostly about how Reg would take his parents' and sister's death. It was easier for him to blame himself for not listening and think they went on to live a happy life.

Babe called Reg downstairs and led him into the formal living room. "Uh, sir, am I in trouble?" The boy fidgeted like he had a mouse in his pants.

The big guy slung a half-cocked sad grin and said no. "I have some difficult information to share with you." He paused, "After hearing your story, something didn't ring true to me, so I chased it down," Reg interrupted, saying it was true. "Yes, your story was true. What I learned will be hard to hear, but know we are here for you. We think of you as ours." He paused. Reg was sitting on the edge of his chair. He nodded. Babe cleared his throat, "Your parents didn't abandon you at the Aquarium when you were ten; a hit-and-run driver collided with them. They died. That's why they didn't come for you."

Reg's bottom lip and chin began to quiver. Babe gave him the article he had stashed away in a chest of drawers. The boy looked at the picture for what seemed an eternity, then read the article. He broke down sobbing, 'Ellie, my funny little Ellie.' Babe's gut clenched into a tight ball, and a vice grip torqued his heart. Then it happened; a tear rolled down his cheek. "Reg, I'm so sorry." He sniffled and dried his eyes. "Mays is going to handle all the legal stuff. Everything your dad and mom had belongs to you, and

I think, but not certain yet, that your dad's sister—"

Reg blurted, "Fucking Elloise. Mom didn't like her, and she and I used to call her Cruelloise DeVille when I was little. Dad never said it, but I don't think he was a fan. She's a fucking bitch. I heard my parents say that they thought she killed her husband for his insurance money. Do they know who wrecked into them? It says hit and run. How can you hit another car so hard to kill the people and drive away? It doesn't make sense, does it?" Babe shook his head no. Mays and Trinity entered the living room, and the four talked with Trinity as support, setting a plan.

Babe would get Max, his contact in the NOPD, to review the records and see if anything ever came up about the other driver. Who identified the bodies? Mays would handle the rest.

Once they hashed through, Babe told Reg that he and Trinity planned to adopt him and Jacob. They weren't discluding Chris, but the eighteen-year-old was almost a grown-ass man. Down deep, he hoped CJ, Chris' dad, would clean up his act, and the two could start a relationship. Even though it had been years, the big guy knew it was possible. Babe and Mays met when Babe was thirty-six and the older forty-six. At that point, both men had settled in their lives, gone there and done that. They, in one short meeting, became close as life-long brothers. Maybe the brothers needed it, and CJ was okay with his chosen life and would not want to rekindle a relationship with Chris. Time would tell, as would a call to Glenn, Bethany's husband and Babe's construction boss. Hopefully, CJ had cleaned up and sought a job with Glenn.

Mays spent the better part of the night researching the life of David Eglin. He was reasonably confident the Will they had was fraudulent, but the document stood since there wasn't anyone to question the validity. Just for shits and giggles, Mays looked up more information about David. He'd graduated from Catholic High in 2005. Mays called to Babe, "Come see this; you won't believe it." He'd found David's high school picture, and there was no doubt that Reg was his son; the images were uncanny. He followed his life into college, and the trail went cold until he looked up old company business documents showing the grandfather and Reg's dad posed for a corporate picture. There must have been a colossal fuck up in Elloise's life that led her to such heinous acts.

Mays referenced the high school yearbook again. The things one could find on the internet were amazing. David Eglin and Stuart Reams, both high school football players, were also best friends—according to one classmate, in fun facts about the graduating class, they were like red beans and rice. Both went to L.S.U. Stuart graduated from law school. *Interesting.* He was a partner with Hutchins, Spears, Daniels, and Reams. He gave it a shot and called the firm, knowing he'd get a recording, which he did. The message said 'press four' to leave a message for Stuart.

"Hello, Mr. Reams. This is Mays Connolly. I have a client, the son of David Eglin, and I could use a few moments of your time first thing in the morning. I have a sit down with Austin Guilbault at nine tomorrow. Hopefully, you'll get this message, and we can meet beforehand. Sorry to call at this ridiculous hour, but I wanted you to get the message first thing in the morning. Thank you."

There was no doubt in his mind that when Stuart took one look at Reg, he'd know it was his best friend's son. He'd learn more from him than anyone else if they connected. He left his phone number in an email. Mays scrolled through documents. Ten minutes after leaving the phone message, his phone buzzed. "Mays Connolly."

"Mr. Connolly, this is Stuart Reams. We need to talk. I can't believe Reggie is okay. I can meet with you at my office at seven-thirty. If need be, I will go to your meeting with you. Austin is a piece of shit and in cahoots with Elloise. I don't know if you've had the pleasure, but I assure you it is not a pleasure. She is a sociopath." The conversation went on for an hour. Mays told him about Babe and how Reg had been on the street. He revealed the whole story. As it was, Stuart had been David's lawyer and had original Wills, property info, and everything one would need for the case. Now, having the actual legatee, Reg, the courts would have no choice but to open a case against Elloise Eglin and Austin Guilbault. Stuart suggested that Babe attend the early meeting as well. He was excited about seeing his friend's son and wanted to thank the man who saved the boy in person.

Bright and early the following day, Babe, Mays, and Reg took off for Baton Rouge to see Stuart Reams. Reg said the name sounded familiar, but he wasn't positive. The man's office was in a renovated warehouse. "This place is the bomb. I hope I remember the dude." Reg excitedly said while Babe and Mays watched the boy pace the reception area. They heard footsteps approaching. The old wooden floors creaked and made an echo effect. The man entered. With eyes as big as saucers, Reg looked over and spoke, "Oh, my God, Stuey." He looked at Babe and Mays, "Fuck, yeah!" Babe cleared his throat. Reg was glowing with excitement. "Y'all, this is my godfather and Dad's best friend, Stuey."

The man choked up and opened his arms to Reg. The two embraced. "I can't believe it's you. Shit, you look exactly like Big Dave." The man was of size, maybe six-foot-one, with a reasonable physique. He looked over toward the two massive men. "Mays?" he inquired. The big blond stepped closer and shook his hand introducing his brother Babe. They both were waiting for a comment baseball reference, but one never came. "Please follow me." They walked down a long hall to the end and a corner office. Being a renovated old building, it featured brick walls and old-fashioned windows.

A table filled with fruit, pastries, and coffee mugs was to the side of the room. Rather than spend time on the hows and whens of finding Reg, he focused on what they were in for with Elloise. Stuart had all the legal documents, including the original Will, with no smudge marks. Babe handed over his guardianship documents.

Mays looked over Stuart's documents. "Gentlemen, this should be a slam-dunk to open a case. The facts are indisputable. Both Reg and El were named beneficiaries." No one wanted to bring up Ellie's death in front of Reg, but clearly, he was the only heir. They would subpoena all documents related to David and Elizabeth. "Fingers crossed the judge will be expeditious. It's already been six years. We should stick to documents and hard evidence and not enter the realm of emotional stress, etcetera; it'll just muddy the water." They all took a minute to feast on the food provided by Stuart. The man kept looking at Reg with glazed eyes. He hugged Reg again and mentioned he was the boy's godfather.

Stuart wanted to hear Babe's story. "We don't have enough time, but I will tell you the sordid tale after we get this ball rolling."

"Y'all, before we head out, I want to make a phone call. He FaceTimed his wife. "I have someone you'll want to say hello to. I don't need to tell you who, you'll know." Stu handed the phone to Reggie. All they could hear was tearful squeals.

"Don't cry, Auntie Barb. I'm fine. As soon as possible I'll come to see you. How are Manda, Betsy-Boo, and Baby Stuey? I imagine he's not a baby anymore." He waited while she excitedly babbled about the shock. "Well, I have to go now, we're going to kick some Elloise ass." They could hear a few controlled giggles, and the conversation ended with her telling him she loved him.

Stuart led the way; Babe followed closely behind. Mays said, "When we get there, I'll have Stuart come in with me, and you and Reg will stay in the reception area or hall. Because we're unsure of the setup, just stay close so you'll be quick when I text you. If it were me, I'd want to lay eyes on Reg, or maybe not." Babe agreed.

Austin's office was in a nondescript fifteen or twenty-story building. The parking attendant gave them a ticket to have validated on their way out of the meeting. Stuart advised, "I know Austin, and he is a schmoozer. Don't talk too much; he's good at needling facts you don't mean to be divulged. He's a snake." The four entered the elevator out of the parking area.

Babe asked what his deal with Elloise was—friends with a twist, perhaps? The few words Stu uttered indicated the affair was scandalous and created quite a stir in the Baton Rouge social scene. Austin's wife was at the center of most boards and fundraisers and had the community more in her pocket than he did. *Good for her,* Babe thought. She had threatened to wipe him out if he didn't cooperate. *Ballsy woman. He will get more than his comeuppance.* Niggling in his mind was how involved the man had been in burning Elloise's parent's house and the hit-and-run vehicular events. More than likely, the parents were already dead inside before the house was set alight, and all evidence went up in the flames.

Mays and Stuart entered the office while Babe and Reg took a seat on a bench by the bank of elevators.

Reg vibrated with nerves. "What's up, little man? Mays has your back and will do nothing to put you in harm's way. It seems Stuart Reams is rather fond of you as well. No worries."

Reg could feel his heart pumping madly in his neck, and he had trouble swallowing as his saliva was beyond viscous. It was all too much. "Sir?" Babe put his arm around Reg's shoulder. "Ya know, I don't care about the money or like their personal things. I would like to know where their graves are. Could we stop at the cemetery on our way back home?" It looked as though the boy was near tears. Babe assured him a stop at the cemetery would happen and felt sure that Stuart knew where to go.

Stuart Reams was a big man at six foot one. Like the bookends, he had a muscular build. It was unfair to compare most people to the brothers, as not many people were as big and muscular as Babe. Mays was getting there. They were formidable. Stuart had a set jaw when they entered Austin's office, whereas Mays had a welcoming smile. Perhaps his good heart and warm Southern charm made him even more lethal in the courtroom; nobody ever expected it. He could slice people off at the knees, and they would say thank you. It was one of those fuck yous that you didn't feel until hours later, and then there wasn't a recourse.

The sweet receptionist offered the men coffee and said Mr. Guilbault would be with them shortly. A thirty-something brunette came from the back. She was all business with a face that looked like it would crack if she smiled. Mays stood, put his hand out, and said, "And you must be Ms. Carney. A good morning to you, ma'am." Nope, no smile.

"I am surprised to see you, Mr. Reams. Mr. Connolly didn't tell me you would be with him." She hurriedly walked with sharp, determined steps. She walked down the hall lined with big wooden doors personalized with name plates and their position or title in the firm. Coming to one of the last ones, she knocked and opened the door. "Mr. Guilbault, Mr. Connolly from Atlanta, and you are acquainted with Mr. Reams."

Mays extended his hand to Guilbault, who stood five foot eight and probably weighed one sixty soaking wet. "Please, it's Mays." Stuart remained silent but threw a devious grin toward the attorney. All three men sat at a table in his office. Austin was condescending when addressing the big blond man. Mays thought, *I'm Southern, not stupid, and you're just as Southern, dimwit.*

"So, am I to understand that you represent Reginald Eglin, Mr. Connolly, uh, Mays? I was under the impression the boy had died. I suppose you have all the necessary documents. I see you don't have the boy with you."

Mays relaxed his hands on the table, "Oh, but I do, sir. I thought we could get through all the legalities before subjecting the poor boy to boring legalese." Guilbault opened a file and pulled out the Will. Mays took it and read through the whole thing. He visibly frowned.

"Austin, may I call you by name, sir?" the man nodded. "If you compare the original document drawn up by Stuart, it is practically identical to the one you have other than paragraph five-a, which is missing from yours. That is where David, Mr. Eglin, bequeaths his ownership in the business, financial holdings, and a quarter of his estate to the boy. Now, it states, should his wife predecease him, or in this case, die in the same incident, then half would go to the living children. Sadly, young Elloise was also a casualty in the event, thus leaving one hundred percent of Stuart's estate to Reginald. The Will is straightforward, without any ambiguity. Where did the proceeds from the sale of their home go? If my math is correct, Mr. Eglin's estate is in the ballpark of eighteen million dollars. We could always include interest, but since it's family, I see no need to complicate the matter. As one can find almost everything on the internet, I took the liberty to locate Ms. Elloise Eglin's net worth. Does sixty-nine million sound about right? Therefore, she should not have any problem settling the matter with Reggie." Guilbault's color was draining, and it looked like he felt ill.

"We would invest his money and have it at his disposal. I assure you we will monitor his investments with express frugality." Mays shrugged a shoulder with an elongated blink and flipped his hand out at the wrist, casually stating, "For things such as cars and education, although the boy will probably not need much with the potential of scholarship. Babe Vicarelli is his legal guardian and has said he will provide for the boy; he has for two years and does not require any compensation. He loves the boy and treats him as a son."

Austin sat with a blank look, not knowing quite what to say. The attorney from Atlanta had everything nailed tight, leaving no wiggle room. Elloise was going to have a meltdown. She had planned things to the tee. Who could have foreseen that a ten-year-old alone on the streets could fend for himself, especially one born with a silver spoon?

Austin took a deep breath, painted a smile on his face, and exclaimed, "Elloise will be ecstatic to know the boy is well. I shall call her directly. I imagine she will want the guardianship transferred from Mr. Vicarelli to her. After all, she is family." Mays knew Babe would never let that happen.

Stuart leaned forward, squinted his eyes in anger, and, dripping with venom, inquired, "And why would she want anything to do with the boy? She took him out of the Will, didn't file a missing child report, and made no effort to find Reggie." He flipped through pages, his eyebrow lifted, and reflected a confident smile. "Actually, Austin, Dave named me as a residential custodian for both children if something happened to him and his wife. I am also Reggie and Ellie's godfather. Big Dave and I were friends closer than brothers from our youth. Which reminds me, I will have to change my directive at some point as I had Dave and Elizabeth named concerning my children." Any confidence Austin had vanished in a heartbeat.

Austin called Elloise; she was too busy to take his call. "Any chance I can meet the boy?" He was trying his best to be friendly. All body movements and facial expressions revealed he was anything but okay. The friendly Atlanta attorney had blindsided him. Little did he know the best was yet to come. Mays knew his brother freaked many people out with his intensity. As jovial as Mays was, Babe was stoic and anything but chatty or friendly, which many found menacing.

Mays texted Babe.

Mays: It's showtime.

Babe: On our way in.

"Sir, I'm nervous. What do I say?" Reg asked.

The big man looked down at him, putting his arm around his shoulder, "You got this, Reg. I got your six."

Reg cocked his head and hiked one side of his top lip up, wrinkling his nose. "Huh?"

"I got your back. I'll explain later. All's good, my young friend. I love you, Reg, and nothing will get in our family's way."

"Whatever it means, I got your six, big guy. I love you, too." Babe chuckled.

The friendly receptionist led them through the door to the desk of a brunette sour puss. If she wanted attitude, Babe could have plenty and scared the crap out of most people. Reg was his typical charming self. He had a full-blown smile and a slight wave of the hand. She ignored his gesture. Babe cleared his throat, "Austin Guilbault." He didn't smile; he just glared with intensity. He wasn't gonna have anybody dis his boy, any of his boys, and Lord help them if they dared to insult the princess. Miss Gloomy Guts opened the door, and the two entered. He stood next to Reg, his hands clasped behind him.

As expected, Babe took Austin down a few pegs just looking at him. He had thought Mays was a big fellow, but the dark man didn't have a warm anything, all badass, and Austin was clearly intimidated. Thoughts swirled through Babe's mind. *I bet he's wishing he hadn't gotten in bed with Elloise.* He looked like a decent person minus a backbone.

Mays stood beside Babe, "Austin, this is my brother, Babe Vicarelli. He is Reg's legal guardian. He's an attorney as well."

"Please, everybody, take a seat," Austin offered. "Mr. Vicarelli, would you get me up to speed and tell me how you became Reginald's guardian?"

Babe breezed past his time in the Corps. He wasn't one to toot his own horn. Mays interrupted and said his brother had been a Captain in the U.S. Marine Corps for years and, upon leaving the Corps, moved back to his home in New Orleans, frequenting the same place for dinner. He came to meet Reg and some of his street kid friends, spotting them a few dollars here and there.

Babe interjected. "The real issue here is that I was able to retrieve young Reg and two other young men from a trafficker, and since I'd seen the boy on the street, I knew he was homeless and took him in. He and the other boys have attended a private school for two years. In all, there are three young men that I have taken in and have full plans of adopting if they desire. I am married, and my wife and I have a baby girl. My large home has plenty of room for young men to grow. I have a full-time live-in house sergeant or governess. Reg is well cared for and loved. I know Mays has provided you with the guardianship documents. Should you have any other questions, please call Reg's attorney, Mays or Stuart Reams. We are working as a team for the well-being of this fine young man." Babe couldn't help but notice Austin trying not to stare at the muscles in his arms, but he glanced back and forth.

The sour puss secretary buzzed. Cruelloise was on the line. Austin quickly picked up the phone. "Good morning to you, as well, Elloise. I had the surprise of a lifetime this morning when your nephew's attornies showed up for the meeting." He lifted his eyebrows, pointing to the phone. Everyone in the room knew who he was talking to. Babe could only imagine the shit fit on the other side of the phone. "Why, yes, the boy is present. It is startling he looks identical to the photos I've seen of your brother. I can see if they can wait while you come to the office. We have some financial issues to handle. I'll give you all the details when I see you." The conversation ended. "Gentleman, when my client arrives, I will need a few moments to speak with her alone. I know this will be an emotional shock for Ms. Eglin, and she might need a moment to collect herself."

Stuart said they'd be agreeable to that, and it was perfectly understandable since Elloise thought Reg was dead. It was like he'd come back to life.

THE BATTLE BEGINS

Reg and his mom couldn't have been any closer to the truth. As though a wake of evil traveled behind her, Elloise had the persona of the villain in a kids' movie. Babe could see why they had called her Cruelloise de Ville. Standing near five-ten in high heels, she was dressed in designer wear and had the red-soled stilettos Trinity was looking forward to wearing again. She had pulled her dark hair tightly into a twist, giving her a severe appearance. She had what looked like two-carat diamond studs in each ear, and her fingers sparkled with bands of diamonds, sapphires, and emeralds. Not that Babe gave a shit, but the woman wreaked money, whether obtained by murder or inheritance, made no difference—it was her expectation in life, no doubt.

Performing a charade of exuberance, she stretched her arms to Reg, who looked at Babe for advice or a bail-out. "Ms. Eglin, Reg isn't the huggy type of lad. Forging his way on the street has made him suspect of strangers." Reg puffed out his chest; Babe had saved the day.

With mini steps, she approached the boy. "Oh, Reginald, you must remember me, your Auntie Wease. Darling boy, you're with family now." Reg was almost the same height as his devil aunt and found it odd that she acted like he was a scared ten-year-old boy.

Reg looked her straight in the eyes and spoke cordially but to the point, "Yes, ma'am. Babe and Trinity Vicarelli are my parents. I'm sorry if I offend you, but I don't recognize you." He stood with a round-eyed look of honest innocence. He played the part to perfection.

She said perhaps with time, he would recall them being together on Thanksgiving. The woman had admitted that she was only with the boy on Thanksgiving—*some aunt.* Babe and Reg stood relaxed but silent—typical for Babe, highly unusual for Reg.

Austin chimed in at the awkward moment of silence. "Let us all have a seat at the table." The man was nervous to the point where he didn't know what he was saying. "Obviously, I have had no time to draw up a document, but I would like a few moments alone with my client. Gentlemen, if you please. He opened the door, and the four of them filed out. *Sit, stand, stay, go, yep, Austin is pissing his pants.*

They called for the elevator and then went out the front door. Stu barked a laugh, "Wow, you rang her bell, Reggie. Do you really not remember her?"

Reg looked the man square in the eyes, "She didn't look like that; boy, she's had some work done. They stretched all the witch wrinkles away." He turned to Babe, "I am not living with that woman. Put me out on the street if you want, but not to her." His eyes got misty. Babe reminded him that he told him he wasn't going anywhere.

Simply put, Reg was part of the family, and they'd have to put up one hell of a fight to take him away. Babe would never let that happen. The boy would be the next casualty on her hit list; maybe that would buy Austin a year or two more.

"You could have given me a head's up, Austin. I feel like a train ran me over." She sat while he worked on the computer, learning more about the two big men. "How much do they want? I shouldn't give that boy a red cent. David said horrible things to me, and shit, if that boy doesn't look just like him. I guess he'll try to put the screws to me. What's the deal with dumb and dumber?"

"Eh, eh, Elloise, neither one of those men is stupid. The blond is a partner in a big firm in Atlanta and has won some noteworthy cases. The Marine could buy both of us out, has been in fierce combat, won medals, and is an attorney in his own right. He does pro-bono for homeless or indigent kids. El, don't fuck with them; I'm warning you. Just cut the check and call it a day." She pulled a cigarette out of her purse. "Not in here." He commanded.

She grumbled. "This is just what I need; it's like my brother has risen from the grave. He's determined to fuck with me. My mother and father had booked and planned a massive wedding for me, and what happened?" She whined. "He knocks up his girlfriend; my wedding gets postponed so they can get married. My brother used to tell me, 'We have to do the right thing, Elloise. Don't be so self-centered and uncaring.' He was a self-righteous prick. Can you believe it; he acted like I was at fault?" She was breathing so hard she rattled. "How much do they want?"

He looked up from the computer, answering, "Eighteen million."

She screeched, "Eighteen million! Like hell. I know what I'm going to do. I'll pay them a tease, follow the money, find out where they live and—"

His jaw dropped, and anger filled his eyes, "You leave them alone. I don't think you want to mess with them."

She paced, playing with the cigarette in her hand. "You are right. I will cut them a check for some money today, but I have most of my funds in investments, as you know. Maybe they will consider payment over time, so I don't get whacked with tax consequences." Austin was skeptical, but she was right; they had to consider tax and legalities. Reg's attorney seemed reasonable and would understand, and Mr. Vicarelli, with his vast wealth, surely understood the financial world and the burdens that could come upon them. For once, Elloise came across with a good idea and not just a tit-for-tat or self-indulgence. He called the bubbly receptionist and asked her to send the group back. She scurried to the elevator and the lobby floor to find them outside the building.

"Oh, there you are. Mr. Guilbault and Ms. Eglin are ready for you now." She led the way, babbling about what a beautiful day it was. Mays struck up a conversation with her while Babe and Reg remained silent. The Marine did not like his feelings upon meeting Ms. Eglin, which set off tingles in his fingertips. She led them to the surly secretary, who led the few steps to Austin's office.

Austin was overzealous, which sent up red flags for Babe. "I hope we didn't keep you too long."

Mays was quick to respond that all was well. Austin presented the proposal to Mays and Stuart; Babe and Reg sat without exhibiting any emotion. The big guy laughed inwardly. It was funny how his boys had learned the art of masking their feelings; he hoped it wouldn't come with his darkness. So far, as he watched them grow, none possessed an evil spirit; in fact, just the opposite, they were loving and kind, even Chris, who tried to act all uncaring and badass.

"Are you okay with that?" Mays asked Babe. He had heard the gist about paying in increments. The money would all be socked away for the boy's adulthood. He'd have Mays and Stuart set it up, keeping distance between Elloise, Reg, and himself. He wasn't one to hit a woman, but if there were ever a woman that needed a thrashing, it was the evil bitch. However, if they were trying to kill him, like psycho Marky, that was a whole different situation.

Babe answered with a single nod. "You and Stu set it up for the boy. Keep me out of it."

Elloise cleared her throat and, with as much sugar as she could muster, suggested, "We will need to get your address, Mr. Vicarelli, to mail the check," then smiled.

"No, ma'am. Mays or Stuart will set it up so you can directly deposit into Reg's account. I see no need for any other interaction." He glanced down at Reg, "Do you?"

"No, sir." The boy didn't even shift his eyes to the woman. Usually, Reg was Mr. Chatty and charming, but clearly, he didn't have any affection for the woman.

Elloise was annoyed. "The boy should reside with me, Mr. Vicarelli. I am his blood. We need to arrange visitation; it's only fair." Mays could see the red rising up the back of Babe's neck and acknowledged her suggestion, pointing out the court had already determined Mr. Vicarelli as legal guardian. There was no point in pushing his intention to adopt; that would show his hand and start a fight unnecessarily. He'd already mentioned it to Austin; whether he heard it or not was questionable. 'Don't ever show your hand, Babe,' he remembered his grandfather teaching. 'It gives you an edge and keeps them guessing.' Elloise was growing more frustrated by the minute. If she exploded, he and Reg would leave, period. She was an underhanded, self-righteous bitch, and Reg was better without her in his life. The meeting would be a one-and-done.

She began to sputter with the beginning of contempt. Babe stood and said, "This meeting is over. Mays and Stuart will handle everything from this point onward. Good day." They turned and walked out.

Reg was candid, "See what I mean, sir, she is bat-shit crazy. It was weird; I got the creeps; I felt like she was out for me. Is that my imagination playing tricks on me?"

Babe swallowed and looked at the boy with his crooked smile, "Reg, welcome to the world of spidey senses. Pay attention to those tinglings; they are your body's warning signal. I did not like the vibes I got from her, so you are probably dead on balls right."

Stu and Mays exited the building ten minutes later, talking and laughing with each other. Babe was waiting to hear her reaction to them leaving. Mays laughingly said, "Brother, you know how to piss people off. That woman would've loved to scratch your eyes out. She does not like you. I'll set up the account in Atlanta, and Stuart will handle any legal issues since he is here. I think she might pay one installment, but she's going to forget," and he used air quotes on forget, "her obligations." Babe smiled and nodded. "Have all your boys learned the power of silence? Ya know it shakes some people up? Ms. Elloise didn't like your stoicism or Reg's."

Babe chuckled, "And who gives a fuck? I'd rather not have anything to do with this, but I feel his dad would want Reg to have his inheritance. I'm convinced she has other money or investments hidden, but whatever. Like Ruthie says, 'Gawd, don't like ugly.'" He imitated the old gal.

Reg asked Stu to direct them to the graves. After what seemed like half an hour, they pulled up to an old graveyard. It had the feeling of days gone by. Stuart gave a guided tour. Some of the tombstones from great-great-grandparents went back to the eighteen hundreds. He stopped at a beautiful headstone with a bouquet of fresh flowers. Reg read the names. It was theirs. "He asked the three men if he could be alone for a minute. They backed away. After five minutes, Babe glanced back; Reg was sitting on the grave, his body pulsating from sobs. Even though he was nearly an adult, he still exhibited childlike ways. He talked to them as though they were there. Calling out to Babe, Reg asked him to come over. Teary-eyed, he stood up as the big guy approached. Babe put his hand on Reg's shoulder. "Mom, Dad, Ellie, this is Babe; he takes care of me and is my dad now. I wanted you to meet him. I'll be back now that I know where you are. I miss you." The two turned and walked away and joined Mays and Stuart. "Who puts the flowers there?"

Stuart smiled, "I do. I miss your dad, and I try to visit once a month. Right after it happened, I was here every day." He blew his nose into a handkerchief. "I loved your dad like a brother and miss him. I'm glad you know where they are, and any time you want to visit, I'll be happy to lead the way." After a few minutes, he spoke again. "If I had any idea that you were alive, I would've hunted you down. I am sorry."

He said Trinity always said everything happens for a reason. The way the cards landed, he felt he was meant to be with Babe and Trinity.

Back at the office, Elloise was seething. "You find out where that boy lives, goes to school, and everything there is about him," she barked. "I feel like they are extorting me." She paced in front of the window as though wearing a path. "I don't care what you say; something is up with that dark-headed monster." She sat at the table, grabbed a pad and pen, and began making instructions for Austin; she grabbed her checkbook out of her purse and made a check out for five hundred thousand. Austin shook his head, telling her she needed to up the ante. She slammed her hand on the check and said that was all she planned on giving. A conversation, more of a disagreement ensued. He had locked himself so tightly with Elloise that he'd never pry loose from her talons.

Elloise became eerily quiet. He knew she was plotting something underhanded. No one said it, but everyone in their inner circle knew Elloise had put the fire in motion to kill her parents and had hired an assassin to kill her husband. The police couldn't prove anything linking her, but anybody who was somebody knew the extent of the woman's depravity. It wasn't a stretch to think she'd orchestrated the death of her brother. Austin played the game well and stayed silent, not disclosing his thoughts. He knew he'd be the next target if he raised a stink.

With a crossed leg swinging to beat the band filled with toxic aggression, she placed a call. "Des, we need to grab a quick lunch today. Are you available?" Austin cleared his throat; she shot a daggered look across the room at him. "I guess tomorrow morning might work if it has to be. How familiar are you with New Orleans? Never mind, I'll see you in the A.M. Yellow Brick." Austin crossed the room and stood in front of her. "What?" she commented in a hate-filled voice, then shrugged a shoulder and purposefully looked away from him. The woman was unscrupulous beyond words, and he knew he needed to keep his opinions to himself, or he'd be the next to have an unfortunate accident. However, she had nothing monetarily to profit from his demise; it would have been for a power trip or hiding evidence. "Meeting over, here's the one and only check. I'm too busy to sit here and have you stare at me disdainfully." She slapped the check in his hand and left the office without another word.

Now that she was gone, he felt compelled to call. "Mr. Connolly, this is Austin, yes, Mays. I feel the only right thing to do is to warn you. Elloise has contacted her hired thug and is sending him to New Orleans, so keep an eye on the boy. I don't know her plans, but she's up to no good."

Mays pointed at Babe, beckoning him closer. He tapped the speaker. "Thank you for that warning. Who is her henchman?" Babe asked.

Austin said the man's name was Des, but he had no idea what he looked like or where he lived. He heard her make plans with him to meet the following morning at the Yellow Brick. Babe gave Mays the thumbs-up, cordially closing the conversation.

The entire way back to the city, the three of them spoke about the weirdness of Reg's aunt. They had a good laugh over Cruelloise. Reg opened up about his parents and his sister. He'd had a happy childhood up until age ten. Babe called Stuart, asking if he knew the whereabouts of the Eglin's furniture or personal belongings. The man knew exactly where they were; he'd rented storage for boxes and the like, but they had sold the house furnished, except for the odd piece, such as a baby cradle and antique high chair. He stated that while David and Elizabeth did well financially, they didn't live to impress. They lived in a comfortable home with down-to-earth furnishings. Big Dave, as he called him, and Elloise were polar opposites. "Stuart, you refer to him as Big Dave. Is there a story behind the name I can share with Reg?"

The man chuckled, saying that David had always been much bigger than him when they were kids. However, in tenth grade, Stu surpassed him by an inch to his current height, but the name stuck. Dave was six feet flat but broadly built. "Not like you, Babe, but along the same lines, just more compact. He was a force to contend with playing on the line in football, though—strong as a fucking ox."

The strained, angry feeling started to pass once Babe developed a plan of action. His muscles had been tense with gripped fists, but the tension began to drain. The following morning, he would return to Baton Rouge alone and use the Mercedes. It was such a nondescript vehicle, given its age. He'd wait down the street from Elloise's house and follow her to the meet. Once he laid eyes on her thug, he'd head back to New Orleans.

After a long day and a plethora of information, they tiredly pulled into the driveway at Chestnut. Babe had taken some pics on the sly, knowing Trinity would want to see all parties involved. She always wanted every detail. The other two boys were most curious about what was going on with Reg. "Reg, how do you want to handle the situation with Jake and Chris? They have been chomping at the bit, knowing something has been going on, and I don't want anything coming between y'all, but it's your story to tell. I'll follow your lead." Babe glanced at him in the rearview mirror. "Just wanted to ask to solidify that before we got out."

Reg shrugged and said, "Sir, they are my brothers. We may not have been born by the same Mom and Dad, but there is no doubt we are. I've already told them some, remember? They've known since forever that my parents left me at the Aquarium. Chris actually helped me a lot in the beginning. I'll tell them everything. But, while we're talking about it, when can I get a car? I'm sixteen and can get my license. I know how to drive; Chris has been letting me drive to school. Now that I have money, I can pay for a car and insurance."

Babe glanced at him with a half-smile. There was no doubt these were his boys. For the most part, they conducted themselves following house rules. They liked the structure and didn't get into drama like he heard them talk about concerning kids in their classes.

The ladies of the house had been in the kitchen with Trinity being the chef and Ruthie an extra set of hands. Crawfish Bisque was a labor of love, but it was one of the meals Trinity had mastered on par with those of famous chefs and restaurants. The house was an aromatic delight tantalizing even the most sophisticated taste buds.

The three entered the house. Mays spoke first, "Something smells killer in here. Bro, you eat like this often? Miss Ruthie, that's some delicious aroma." He walked into the kitchen.

Trinity stood with a hand on her hip, " 'Scuse me? I'll have you know, I prepared this fine meal. It's one of my best dishes." Babe gave her a quick peck and joined Mays towering over the pot. "Vic, does it surprise you that I can prepare haute cuisine?" He grinned. "I have a couple of tricks up my sleeve," she waggled her eyebrows.

"I do now, and I think we should give Ruthie a few nights off from preparing dinner. You do an excellent job." He put his arm around her and asked in all sincerity, "How are you feeling today? You didn't do too much, did you?"

Reg popped his head in and said he had much to tell about their adventure in Baton Rouge. Trinity had ordered all of Chris' dorm bedding and the things he'd need, and she wanted to make dinner about Chris and college but didn't want to interfere with Reg's story. She was all ears and knew the boys would be too. The boy didn't even know she had ordered everything; maybe she'd wait until it came in, and then dinner could be a presentation. The day's events with the attorney and Reg's aunt were a story worth setting everything aside for.

Chris and Jacob sounded like a herd of animals coming down the stairs. Trinity hollered for them to slow down. Each filled their bowl and headed to the table Ruthie had set, complete with a bread basket at each end. Trinity gave a heartfelt grace, and they dug in with many compliments. Reg was more hyper than usual, wanting to tell the story word by word, action by action, without missing a single beat. "Y'all shoulda seen these two big guys; my aunt, Cruelloise de Ville, was shut down and fast. First, I got to see Stuey, that's what everyone called him; he was my dad's best friend. Between him and Uncle Mays, I have the best attornies ever. Y'all know how nice Mays is that even if he's telling you off, you can't help but say thank you." The whole table agreed with a laugh. "Man, they took over the meeting, and when Cruelloise came in, she didn't know what to say." He went on for forty-five minutes, hardly taking a breath. "And then the best part. I got to see where they buried my mom, dad, and sister." The tears started to trickle down his face. "A hit-and-run driver killed them, y'all. They didn't leave me, but now I know for sure I have them looking over me." He sniffled. The other two boys got choked up, as well. While the boys had seen a rough side of life, it only made them more appreciative, and they knew Babe had spared them a life of sheer Hell.

Ruthie dabbed her eyes. "I knew there had to be more to the story. You got ya own personal angels, honey, so you best mind your manners 'cause they're gonna watch after you but also see the mischief you get into. So, remember, when you're cursing like a Marine, they hear you." Everyone at the table looked at Babe, who raised his eyebrows at the old gal. It broke the sorrow with laughter and finger-pointing, all in jest. For better or worse, they were a family.

WHAT GOES AROUND

Bright and early the following day, Babe and Mays headed to Baton Rouge, hoping to lay eyes on Des, Cruelloise's thug. Trinity opted to stay home and out of the picture. The drive provided a chance for the brothers to map out a plan to thwart any attempts to kidnap Reg and what measures they would need to take to ensure his safety.

Stuart, Reg's godfather, set up an investment account for the boy. Any withdrawal over one thousand dollars would require two signatures, Mays' and Stuart's. "Babe, I'm going to fly home tomorrow. I'm working on a massive case, but I thought I might return for an elongated stay in New Orleans once I wrap up all the cases I have. Would that cramp your style? My most significant consideration is how it will affect my mom and dad. I think the kids will roll with it, but if they don't, I won't. The grands aren't getting any younger." They parked a half block away from Elloise's house. It was a grand estate, to say the least. She barreled out the driveway, hardly looking for oncoming traffic like she owned the street.

Babe followed closely but remained undetected. She jumped on the interstate and took off like she was at the races. "Look at this shit!" he exclaimed. "We won't catch her without drawing attention, but keep sight of her if you can." Babe wove in and out of lanes of traffic. Mays caught sight of her getting off in Denim Springs, heading toward Highway one ninety. She went a short distance with a few lefts and rights and pulled up to a breakfast brunch place called Yellow Brick House. Hanging outside, dragging on a cigarette, was a dark-haired Hispanic-looking man. Babe parked a half block down and, using binoculars, could see the details of the man's face. No doubt he was from south of the border. He took a few photos. "I'm going to send these to Javier. I know I told you about him. If this guy is the real deal, Javi may know of him, but if he's penny-ante, then maybe not. At least I might be able to get a read on the guy. I wonder if he was the one she used for all her deadly endeavors." Parked in front was a black crotch rocket; Babe laid odds that the thrill machine belonged to Des. Elloise moved with wild animation, flailing arms and a foot stomp like a petulant child.

The two men sat patiently in the car, anticipating Des would soon mount the cycle. The plan was to follow and force him into their vehicle once the coast was clear unless his place was close. Then, it would be time for him to talk.

The man put out his hand, waiting for an envelope of cash. Elloise hemmed and hawed and then handed it over. He pointed to her, hopped on his mean machine, and took off. Babe was right behind him. He took several turns and ended up on a gravel road leading to a trailer park. Babe waited for him to pull in, get off the bike, and enter the trailer. They parked near another trailer. "Mays, stay here and get in the driver's seat." The big blond man slid in, warning him to leave if it got too hairy.

Babe quietly walked to the front door and knocked. He heard the person inside engage his gun. Slowly, the door opened. "Yeah? You got the wrong address. I don't know you." He had a slight Spanish inflection but had been in the States long enough to lose most of his accent—a voice called from inside the trailer. Des responded, "I got this, Ramon. As I said, Mister, you got the wrong address."

Babe had his hands relaxed by his sides. "Do I now, Des?" The Hispanic man shifted from one foot to another. "I don't care about the money; I want information. What did Elloise instruct you? Let me see the envelope." The man reached to the back of his pants, Babe supposed for the cocked gun. "Don't pick a fight you can't win, and not good to cock a gun and stick it in your pants," he winced.

"You got a death wish, asshole?" He pulled the gun out of his pants and brought it around. In an instant, Babe had it turned on the man. He began to stutter, surprised at the swift movement of the massive man. "You say you don't care about the money and only want information?" Babe emptied the chambers and handed the gun back to the man. "What do you want?" He pulled the envelope out of his pants, removed the warm, sweaty money, and handed the envelope to Babe. "It's all here. Picture of a kid, an address in Baton Rouge, a picture of a man with instructions. She wants to adios them."

Babe looked the man straight in the eyes with his empty glare. It rattled the punk. "The boy is my son, and the man is his attorney. I don't know if she hired you to smoke her brother, husband, and parents, and what's more, I don't care, but you fuck with my boy, and you won't know what hit you. That is a promise. What are the plans for the boy and his attorney?" Des was getting jittery. No doubt the big man meant business. True, she'd paid him handsomely throughout the years, but his only worries were the police. The circumstances had taken a sharp turn, and the message he got was loud and clear from the massive stranger. "If I see you anywhere around my boy, you're a dead man. Do you understand?"

"Uh, uh," the man started trippin'. "Look, I'm just gonna back out. I'll call her right now in front of you. I don't need this shit." The man's voice was erratic, trembling with fear.

Babe grabbed the back of the man's neck and pulled him from the trailer. "Don't work that way. Tell her you'll have the boy the day after tomorrow. Up your ante with her and set the meet for ten at Yellow Brick. You better be there at nine-thirty. Remember, I know where you live, and I don't play." Desmond Cruz said he'd be there. It would appear to be some kind of dumb trickery if he didn't show.

What was the plan going to be? Fact: He had to get rid of the aunt. Fact: He had to let Stuart know to back away and keep his mouth shut. Perplexed, his mind wandered, and he questioned why he wanted his boys to understand the severity of going down the wrong road. He didn't want them to look at him as a killer but wanted them to understand the consequences of bad decisions. It was time to step away from the train of thought, but one thing for certain: the aunt was a done deal. Precious Reg needed solace in retribution for the needless murders of his family. The entire trip back to New Orleans, Babe was silent—entangled with his thoughts and rebuttals. Mays respected the quiet and drove the car in silence.

Trinity saw his vehicle pull in, and the two big men exited. Wishing she had been a fly on the wall, she was most curious and questioned every minute detail. Babe was even more reflective than usual, so she backed away, knowing he'd talk when ready.

Babe changed into his workout attire and headed into the garage. Chris was already whaling on the heavyweight bag. "What's up, Chris? You got some pent-up angst?"

Chris stopped short, "Sir, I think I want to join the military. I realized college wasn't for me when I watched how geekafied some of my classmates were. I thought it was, but now, not so much. You've given me this dope opportunity to live the dream, ya know, go to college, go Greek, but in all honesty, I want to make a difference like you." He sat next to Babe on the trunk of the car. "That's all everyone can talk about. Who's pledging, and what dorm? Hell, I don't have a clue what I'd major in." He started taking off his boxing gloves.

"Leave 'em be. To make the most impact, change your stance and follow through with your weight. It'll help you stick the blow." Babe finished putting on his gloves and demonstrated. "Kid, you're getting cut. How much you lifting now?"

Chris answered, "I'm benching 350," a substantial increase from their last conversation.

"You don't have to decide right now to sign up. Try college, but if you are absolutely certain you don't want to go, then your mind is made up. I went to college because I had a wrestling scholarship. Far, my grandfather guided me. Following his advisory role, I think you ought to give it a try. If you don't want the Greek life, don't do it. It wasn't my idea of a good time. All anyone wanted to do was get drunk and laid. Don't like the idea of being drunk and getting laid was never a problem." Babe shrugged a shoulder.

Chris practiced a few more times, and each time, Babe said, 'Better, go again.'

They called it quits and headed inside. Babe went straight to the shower. Trinity watched as he undressed. "Tell me about the adventure," she double-raised her eyebrows. "And did you notice I can do two steps now? I have to hold the railing tight. I sometimes get a little wobbly and off-balance." She had mastered walking on a flat surface. As he stepped into the shower, he took her hand and gently pulled. "Wait, my clothes will get wet."

He grinned, "then, we'll put them in the dryer."

Ruthie called upstairs, saying dinner was ready. Mays didn't hear the old gal; the computer occupied his attention in the study. Ruthie cleared her throat as she approached the room. "Sir, you need to come to the table."

"I'll be right there, ma'am." He continued tapping away on the keyboard, determined to finish his last thought. The case he was working on mirrored the debacle with Reg and his aunt; only the crime was embezzlement, not murder for monetary gain. Mays contemplated that had Babe not been raised by Gino Vicarelli, he would have turned out different, but there wasn't one thing he would change. Although without a full confession, he knew his younger brother had taken lives, and not just in combat. Babe bore the pain of righting the wrongs and protecting the innocents. No, he wouldn't change that; he knew his brother was a good man. Mays finished his thought and took his seat at the dining table.

Trinity could barely sit still; she envisioned Chris' enthusiastic reaction. Babe had not discussed Chris' thoughts about school versus the military. She winked at him and cleared her throat. FedEx had been swift, and the boxes arrived that day, perfect for a celebration. "Chris, close your eyes; I have a surprise for you." She brought boxes from the laundry room and stacked them before him. Babe motioned for her to stand by him. He whispered, "Great ideas. Don't get offended if Chris says he might not attend college. He mentioned the military to me but is going to give college a try. Just a head's up."

"Open your eyes," she excitedly said. "You now have everything any college student could want for a dorm room." He looked through the boxes with an ear-to-ear smile. Chris responded cheerfully, volleying glances with Babe.

Mays returned home with Babe's advice to visit NOLA more often as he and Trinity would visit Atlanta. New Orleans wasn't Buckhead and was getting more dangerous by the day. He didn't want his niece and nephews in New Orleans, fearing they'd go down the wrong street. The conversation would hold until the long ass flight to Norway. After Mays was gone, Babe focused on planning the death and disposal of Elloise. While most of his threat terminations were spontaneous, Elloise's demise would take planning, like Commander Deary.

Babe arrived early at the Yellow Brick establishment, waiting for Des and then Elloise to show. Just the thought of their termination sent an electrified buzz through his body. It gave him time to think about the situation. Fact: The aunt was non-negotiable he'd make sure of that. His disdain for her paralleled a similar opinion he had of Gino, his sperm donor—he didn't harbor one guilty feeling about serving justice. Fact: Anyone who would kidnap a person or animal, for that matter, didn't deserve to breathe; however, Des had no plans of harming Reg, changing the dynamics. Babe internally argued he had to punish the threat to society because he was certain Elloise wasn't his only client, meaning there was an assortment of victims out there unawares.

Des motored in front of the café, skeptically peering in the window. He spotted the big man and entered. "You told Elloise you had the boy?" Babe evaluated any micro-expressions or subconscious body language.

Understandably, Des was jittery, his nerves frayed. He knew the man in front of him could take him out easily. "Yeah, man, I told her I had the kid at my place, and Ramon was guarding." *Hm, collateral damage.* "I told her I didn't want to risk being seen, ya know? She didn't want to come to my crib, but I told her it was the only way. Who knows, man, maybe she might try to kill me; that's why I told her Ramon was playing watchdog. She might not get no ideas, ya know? The lady is a walking death trap. She blazed her parents' house. Man, that's cold-blooded." He ordered coffee and fiddled with the packets of sugar, anything to avoid looking at the massive man. "You gonna end her?"

Babe sat still and silent, shrugging one shoulder and tipping his head to the right. He didn't answer the question, which was unnerving. After fiddling with the sugar, he cracked his knuckles and seemed to do anything to avoid the big guy. "Tell her to follow you. I'll be waiting inside your place."

"Man, I'll let Ramon know. He don't like strangers coming up in our place. Ya know, he's sharing rent; it's not like we're together. I ain't that way. I like a hot piece of ass." He moved his hands in front of him, forming the curves of a woman. Babe raised an eyebrow but said not a word. He was done hearing the nervous rambling of Des.

"I'll be waiting." Babe stood and left.

As Babe pulled up to Des' trailer, a scrawny dark-haired man came out onto the porch with a gun tucked in his pants, resting his hand on the piece. He had a surly punk-ass expression, squinting his eyes for drama and looking Babe up and down. The big guy exited his vehicle and walked toward the trailer. Ramon pulled his shoulders back and puffed out his chest. Babe breezed by him and heard as the little man pulled his gun out. "You're barking up the wrong tree, Poncho," he said as he continued to walk to the trailer.

"Tough guy, I got my piece aimed at you. Show some respect."

Babe closed his eyes, took a deep breath, faced the man, and said in a low voice, "You have to earn it. Don't pick a fight you can't win." The man waggled the gun at Babe, holding it sideways like a wannabe gangster. Swiping his foot, the Marine knocked the weapon from the man's hand. Ramon's face blanched. Babe calmly picked up the gun and pointed it toward the wannabe. He'd had enough and pulled the trigger. He picked up the dead body, trying to avoid any blood spatters, and threw it into the woods.

The television was on a game show. Babe stood in the nasty kitchen, careful not to touch anything. He'd had enough of the bullshit and games. Civilians were a pain in his ass. He heard the motorcycle pull in and Elloise's car right behind. He held great disdain for her and the evil that exuded from her. It'd all be over in a minute.

The woman ran her mouth with constant bitching at Des. She burst into the room, heading to the left and Des' bedroom, expecting to have Reg under her control. The man was right behind her. Not finding the boy, he heard her screech at Des. She came out of the bedroom in a fury, holding a small pistol. She looked at the big man with contempt. He shot, pop one down, pop again, two down. Eventually, someone would find the rotting corpses. Ballistics would prove Elloise's pistol did not claim any of the lives, but Ramon's would long be at the bottom of a bayou, never to be found or certainly not linked to the Baton Rouge trailer park murders. He was done and ready to book flights for Norway. Once again, there was no remorse, complete lack of emotion. He did what needed doing, and that was the end of it.

The whole saga was over and his family could live peacefully. It was his to do, and he executed the mission efficiently and with little drama.

Trinity was waiting at the door for him as he arrived home. "You are a welcomed sight. How'd it all go with the aunt?"

Babe pecked her lips and commented, "As planned and problem solved."

"It must have gone well because you, Big Man," she poked him. "Seem calm, cool, and collected like you're at peace. Chris is in the garage." Babe frowned, his eyebrows furrowing.

"Why isn't he at school? Something wrong?" The concern registered on his face.

She rolled her eyes, "You crack me up." She smiled as she poked him in the ribs. "They are on senior days now and only go half a day for the week, and then that's it. Boy, they have something every day— award programs for sports and academics, mother-son breakfast, father-son lunch on a different day, and graduation followed by a trip to Orlando." She took his hand, "I'm surprised he hasn't mentioned it to you. You've long signed the permission for Orlando and cut the check. It was at the beginning of the year." She pulled him. "C'mon, I'll go with you. He has something to show you, so do not burst his bubble. You hear me?" He went to pick her up to go down the brick steps, but she waved him off, saying she had it. His curiosity was piqued, and he cautiously watched as she navigated the steps.

Chris was glistening with a film of sweat. "Good to see you, sir," Babe observed the changes in the boy. His pecks were impressive, and his washboard abs remarkable. His bangs dripped down his face. Chris was about five feet ten or eleven inches and had worked hard to build his body. "When you get time, I want you to show me some self-defense moves. I'm not expecting to need anything like that, but you never know. I've been in a couple of fights, but I was terrible. I'd probably gotten my ass kicked, but each time someone broke it up." It took him a moment to slow his breathing. "Shit, do you get winded?" Chris turned to get his hand towel. Placed between his shoulder blades was a tattoo of a cross. At least he had the good sense to have a professional do his artwork.

Babe cleared his throat. "When did you get the ink? I don't remember you mentioning it to me. The others know about it?" Chris replied that they knew he wanted one but didn't know he'd gotten it. Babe said he would've liked to know before, but it was his body, and he was a grown-ass man. Chris tilted his head to his shoulder with a face filled with curiosity. He didn't even think Babe would mind since he had some ink. One side of the man's mouth drew back with a smile. "Each one has meaning—Different stages in my Marine journey. The tattoo artist did a good job on your cross. Anything symbolic about it?" Babe noticed a few tears run down Trinity's cheeks. "What's up, ma girl?"

"Chance" was the only word she mentioned. Babe's brows raised as he nodded.

"I was gonna put his name in the center, but thought it might look, well, gay. I mean, I don't care if other people are; obviously, I love Jacob." Babe turned his head toward Trinity. Jake's sexuality had never come up before. After a brief thought, it dawned on him that Jake never talked about girls, and he wondered if he might have issues since being trafficked. It was bound to create confusion. Trinity nodded like she knew. "He might be bi, I don't know, and it's none of my business. Everyone knows Reg is a natural-born horndog."

For the following week, it was one celebration after another. It was the morning of the mother-son breakfast. Trinity donned one of her favorite short black skirts with a gold top and blazer to match the skirt. She wanted to wear her favorite black pumps but didn't feel stable enough, so she wore a pair of sophisticated sandals with a slight wedge heel. She rode most of the way down on the lift chair, stopped it, and carefully descended six stairs. Babe whistled, "Ma girl, you are too hot for such an occasion. Do you have any idea what thoughts you might provoke in those sex-craved young men?" He half-laughed but had other thoughts, like carrying her back up the stairs. "You look outstanding. Have a good time with our boy." He watched them from the porch.

Chris walked her to the car, and off they went. He was unusually reserved, as if something was on his mind. Trinity told him to spill it. "Is it okay if I call you Mom? Nobody at school knows my story; they think I'm like everyone else."

She squeezed his hand. "I'd be honored, Chris."

When they walked into the gymnasium, most of the guys from his class ogled Trinity. He'd already set in his mind that he wouldn't put up with any MILF kind of statements. He knew she was beautiful but couldn't imagine looking at her in such a light. While he didn't call her mom, that's precisely the best way to describe her.

As usual, Trinity could talk to anyone and create conversations while making new acquaintances left and right. It was the gift of a talented bartender. Chris introduced her to the boy he was rooming with, and she and the boy's mom hit it off right from the start. Since the boys would be going to Baton Rouge on the same day, Trinity arranged for his parents, her, and Babe to get an early dinner after getting the boys settled. She'd give her big man no choice. Patrick and Chris chased looks between them.

"Mom," Chris said, "I'm hitting the head, excuse me." Patrick awkwardly stayed behind. Girls could go to the bathroom together, but not cool to ask a guy. While taking a whiz, a couple of boys entered the bathroom. *Here we go*, Chris thought. He knew a comment about Trinity was getting ready to surface. She didn't look like most of the moms. There were many pretty mothers, but not what any of them would consider hot. Trinity was different. She stoked the heat by just being herself.

"Dude, your mom is smokin'." *Passable.* Chris smiled.

Then, one of the other boys, a total jackass with zero class, said, "I never knew you were a half-caste." His tone was demeaning. *Ignore.*

Patrick came in at the perfect moment. The boy repeated the comment to Chris' roommate, who told him to shut up. *Stick the punch with your weight and follow through.* He could hear Babe's words. One more insult and Chris planned to knock the shit out of him, one punch on his way out the door. The guy came out with a doozy as Chris started to exit, and without warning, he stuck a fierce gut punch on the obnoxious kid, who bent over choking. The others in the bathroom told the asshole he got what he deserved.

Once back at the table, Patrick commented under his breath, "Dude, you're a beast." Chris' stomach did flips, proud of how he handled things. No cussing him out or bitch slappin'—one solid plant in the gut. Even though she pretended not to hear, she heard. It would be a conversation going home. He couldn't wait to tell Babe.

Walking to the car, Trinity linked her arm to his. "Are you a beast? Do tell." She squeezed his arm with hers. "I like Patrick's mother. Nice lady. I'm waiting." She looked up at him.

"In the car," he stalled, knowing she wouldn't let up until he explained. They got to the car, and she took off her jacket. "Thank God you didn't do that at breakfast." She shifted her body with a wrinkled forehead and tucked chin, then asked him what he meant by that. "Trinity—"

"I like Mom much better," she blushed.

He laughed, "Okay, Mom, when I went to take a piss, one guy came in and said you were smokin'. That was okay. You probably gave most of the guys a boner looking at you. I was waiting for the MILF, but this one guy, a real piece of work, to coin Babe, said I was a half-caste. I didn't say a word. I finished my piss, and he said it as I was walking out. He was a douche. I punched him in the gut, just like Babe taught me. The kid probably lost his breakfast."

She thanked him for standing up for the family. "You tell them you're Creole. You got more of the French than the Haitian." She giggled like a teenage girl. "Some people are just plain stupid. We had a snotty customer at Louie's who used to call me a little nigga bitch. If Babe had heard that, Mercy Lord, as it was, the guy had a heart attack or something like that and died waiting in line at the bar. That's kizmit."

Chris pulled up to the house. He couldn't wait to tell Babe. He anxiously waited to make sure Trinity made it up the brick stairs to the porch and inside. Then he sprinted, calling out, "Sir, Sir." Babe came from the kitchen. "You're not gonna believe this shit. When I took a piss, I figured one of the guys would come in and make some comment about Trin, um, Mom. There was a lot of wood at the breakfast when they saw Mom. I said to myself, there better not be any MILF talk or any sexual, or I'd make them pay. One said she was smokin', that was okay, but this douche says," he changed his voice. "I didn't know you were half-caste.' I didn't say anything. Then, as I walked out almost to the door, he said it again, and I stuck him with an excellent gut punch. Just like you told me." Babe's eyes opened a little wider, and he nodded.

"I get it. What I failed to tell you was some people seek retribution, especially since you did it in front of other guys and humiliated him. We will wait until all three of y'all are home, and I'll hold Vicarelli Self-Defense 101. It's about time y'all know how to defend yourself, only as a last measure."

RULES OF ENGAGEMENT

Three-thirty rolled around, and it was apparent Chris had boasted about the morning's happenings because Reg and Jake were all about getting outside for Vicarelli Defense Training 101. Trinity was not thrilled at the prospect of Babe teaching violence to the boys but understood keeping peace through strength. The city had become a much more in-your-face environment, and uptown was even more so than the Lakefront where she grew up. Babe explained that much of the exercise was about optics and awareness, not suggesting that the boys look for fights.

Jacob did rabbit punches in the air. Babe scrutinized, "Boy, keep your fists as they are and come here. Do you see how your thumb is sticking out? That, my friend, is a broken thumb in the making, and talk about a bitch of a break. Tuck it down, never, and I mean never, inside your fingers, but like this." Babe held his fist tight and turned it over so Jacob could see the bent thumb over the fingers. Reg rounded the corner. "Reg, come here and make a fist." The boy did as instructed and had it right. "Let's go outside."

Babe and the three boys exited to the backyard as Trinity, with baby in arms, and Ruthie watched from the family room windows. "I know you don't like the idea of the boys fighting, but what your husband is doing is a good thing. I don't need to tell you how dangerous it can be on the streets. I think of my Clive; those punks almost killed him." Trinity acknowledged the comment.

Babe started his teaching by discussing avoiding a fight, which was not exactly what the boys wanted to hear. After a fifteen-minute discussion on the downfalls of fighting, he moved on to the instructions.

The first exercise concerned face-to-face. "Some say make a pre-emptive strike, meaning you will be the first punch, while other fighters want to establish the pros and cons of their opponent. Stay at a distance, arm's length, and attain a good weight distribution; you sure as shit don't want to get knocked down. Fighting on the ground is not the way to go; you can accomplish it, but it is not your first choice. Step in and raise your elbows, locking the opponent's arms, which takes them out of the fight." They practiced on each other. He explained that hitting with an elbow or heel of the hand is effective and desirable—any bony area, like a knee.

Babe told Jake to stand in front of Reg and for the older to start bullying him. Jacob said, "Hey, leave me the fuck alone, asshole. I don't want to fight." He looked at Babe for approval. "Sir, is that what I should say?" Then he asked Babe what he usually said.

He smiled and said in a calm but warning voice, "Don't pick a fight you can't win." His eyes twinkled as though joking, but the boys knew he was serious.

Wide-eyed, Jacob asked, "Have you ever lost a fight?"

Babe turned his head, thinking, "When I know the other person has the upper hand like they have a gun on me or there are five of them, I don't fight but use the time to let the other guy or guys feel superior and plot out my next move. Y'all have to remember, I'm trained and by, in my estimation, the best. Most importantly, don't be the one to pick a fight. Also, if you find yourself in a fight, anything goes—pick up a two-by-four. Dig your thumbs in eye sockets. You fight to stay alive, and sometimes that means the other person gets hurt or maybe even dies." Silence. The three looked at him on the edge of a question they didn't want an answer to. "But, boys, while rare, I have been overpowered a couple of times. It's usually some sort of pussy-move, like throwing a snake in my shower or using a stun gun. Story for a later date." The boys gawked, waiting for him to reveal killing someone.

Babe spoke first. "Yes, I have killed people before and before you ask, not just in war." He stopped for a moment and sighed. "Nobody wins when a life is taken. If someone threatens or hurts one of my people, they pick the fight, and I will take it to them by any means I can." Silence.

Chris asked, "Can you tell us one time? Promise to keep it between us."

Babe didn't answer but stood in front of Chris. He showed him how to position himself and use the heel of his hand to strike the nose or bend at the knuckle and go for the throat. "It'll give you time to get the fuck out of there or prepare to fight. Another way to buy time is to pull the person's shirt over their head. It incapacitates them for five or ten seconds." He looked at Reg, "Let's say you have a girlfriend you like, like big-time. You see another guy drag her into the bushes or a room and try to have their way with her." They simultaneously cocked their heads. "Rape her." All eyebrows raised, and they got it. "What would you do? Right there and then?"

Reg flared his nostrils and snorted like a bull, "I'd pick up whatever the fuck I could find and hit them over the head, and if I couldn't find anything, I'd jump on their back." Babe nodded.

"You, Jacob?" Babe raised one eyebrow. He knew Jacob had been on the street longer than the other two, being born to a drug-addicted working girl. The boy had seen much.

"I'd look in the trash or on the street, grab a bottle, break it, and stab them in the neck. If it were in the park or somewhere, I'd grab a stick and do the same thing." The other two boys dropped their jaws.

"Sounds like a good plan, Jake," Babe replied. "Have you ever hurt anyone, Jake?" The boy looked at the ground. "You can say it, we're family. Don't get the impression that I want you to hurt people. You'd be fighting for someone who couldn't fight." Babe cleared his throat. "I have. A sick fuck kidnapped Trinity, hurt her, and I broke his neck, then ditched the body where they had a bunch of burnt-out cars." Chris and Reg stared blankly. "If anybody tried to hurt one of y'all, I'd do the same thing, but remember, I know how." Babe went over leg swipes, the importance of keeping a plan close to themselves, and not telling the offender things like they'd bust their mouth or beat the pulp out of them. He reminded them usually, those braggarts are the ones that get the crap beat out of them. Silence is king, he stressed.

Jacob admitted that even though he was a little kid then, one of the johns came to the place where some of the girls lived with him and his mom's closest friend, Bunny. Nobody was at the apartment but him and Bunny. The guy started slapping her around, and Jacob said he picked up a wooden chair and hit the man over and over. *Hm. That sounds familiar*, Babe thought. He said the guy left and never came back.

The other two snickered and said he guessed the guy didn't return with a psycho kid in the place.

Babe complimented Chris about not threatening the dick in the bathroom, just taking care of business. Once again, he reminded him about the possibility of retribution. After two hours of instruction, he ended part one of Vicarelli's Self-Defense 101, reminding them to practice with the heavyweight bag.

Trinity called them inside.

A new day dawned in the crazy Senior festivities, "Babe, you have to talk with people at lunch with Chris. Don't just sit there like a big bump on a log. Also, he will probably ask you if he can call you dad, but maybe not." She slid out of bed, went to their closet, and pulled out a blue polo shirt and dark jeans. His stomach tickled at the thought of her dressing him. "You'll look nice, not too dressy, but not too casual, and—" she raised an eyebrow with a sexy grin, "That shirt emphasizes your muscles. I dare say there won't be anyone with your fantastic body. Speaking of—" She climbed on his lap. "Ooh, boy, I love your body, especially when it does magic tricks." He broke into laughter.

"Is that what you call me wanting you? It's a magic trick. I guess, then, abracadabra."

Chris' body was developing from boy to man. He had definition in his musculature, and it crossed the big guy's mind that he had watched him go from a scrawny, filthy boy to a man with class and substance. "Have you decided how you want to introduce me?" Babe questioned.

The boy laughed, and his voice was noticeably deeper. "That is up to you, sir. I want to call you my dad, but you decide." Babe wasn't one to get all sentimental, but it rang the bell in his heart when Chris referred to him as Dad.

They pulled up to the school. "That works," Babe half-smiled. They entered the gym. The first thing was sticky name tags. Being slick, Babe wrote Chris' Dad and stuck it on his shirt. "How's it look?" He chuffed a sarcastic laugh. Chris gave him two thumbs up.

The headmaster approached them and put out his hand to Babe. "Captain Vicarelli, thank you for your service. My name is Ernest Fox, the headmaster. I'm a friend of Jack Kennedy and have heard stories about you. We have enjoyed having your son, Chris, at our school. He's quite a leader and has the respect of his classmates. Will he follow you into the Marine Corps?" The man had a genuine smile and a natural warmth but a commanding voice.

"Coach Kennedy was a mentor to me. He was why I joined the Corps after Law School." Babe stood with his hands resting on his hips, thumbs tucked in the front pockets. "It's a small world," the big guy concluded. *How trite.*

The headmaster said that Jack had been at the school the day before and spied Chris' mother. Thus, the story unraveled, and he commented on what a stunning lady Trinity was. Babe smiled and nodded. He claimed Reg was one of his favorite students, even though he shouldn't admit that.

The boy was charismatic and entertaining, to say the least, but asked about Jacob with concern. All Babe could say was that he was a thoughtful young man and took after him being the silent type. Both men tilted their heads in acknowledgment with a raise of an eyebrow. Most diplomatically, the headmaster mentioned he was aware of the circumstances behind the three boys, not that anyone else knew, and they certainly didn't reflect their pasts. He noted all three were respectful and well-mannered.

"Thank you for saying that, but they better be. We have what I call a house sergeant. Ruthie runs a tight ship and makes those boys follow her rules. I couldn't have anyone better to help my wife and me with the boys and our daughter. I don't want to monopolize your time, sir. It was a pleasure to meet you. Tell Jack I pass on my regards next time you see him." They shook hands, and Babe turned to walk off. The man lightly grabbed his arm, asking if he knew Jack was sick. Babe's gut dropped, and his heart had a vice-like squeeze. No, he hadn't heard. *Shit.* The headmaster suggested Babe give him a call.

Chris and Babe sat at the table with other students and their dads. As predicted, the topic of discussion ranged from the Corps to Babe's build and how it looked like Chris was following in his footsteps with his build. The torture didn't last long as the school served food and said grace. Silence fell in the room as everyone ate.

All Babe could think about was Jack Kennedy. The man had meant the world to him and had been the ideal role model. The feeling of someone taking his side for once carried him through the tough times in high school. The establishment always thought he was at fault because he was the bigger kid. Jack was the first to sit in Babe's corner and say no. While the big kid could have beaten the living snot out of any of the boys who harassed him in high school, he didn't, and Jack saw it, perhaps why he recruited him for the wrestling team. Being the wrestling coach and a tough son of a bitch, created the goal for Babe. One day, he'd be a Marine like Jack, and he was.

Reed, one of the dads at the table, said, "What is your name? I see you're Chris' dad, but what name do you go by?" *Here we go again.*

"Babe Vicarelli." Silence engulfed the table.

Chris chirped in fast before someone said something they'd regret. "My great-grandfather was from Norway, and he thought America was the best country in the world cuz it is. He loved baseball, America's favorite pastime, or at least to him. He named my dad after Babe Ruth and my uncle Mays after the great Willie Mays."

One of the boys, Tommy Glass, exclaimed, "That is so cool. Is your brother as big as you?" He asked the big guy. Babe grinned, thinking of when he first met Mays—big and pudgy.

Babe wasn't used to the inconsequential bullshit banter, but Chris was beaming with pride, so Babe answered, "Close. We're the same height—"

Filled with excitement, Chris answered, "My mom calls them bookends, so they're close, but my Uncle Mays has blond hair. He talks a lot more than my dad." *Swallow the compliment so it sticks,* per Trinity. His chest tightened, holding back his over-the-top emotions. Babe was doing this for Chris but was more than ready to leave, becoming increasingly uncomfortable.

The headmaster soon wrapped up the lunch with a rambling dissertation about the young men and how they were embarking on a journey, making their mark on the world. The adventure ended with a quick prayer, and the room of testosterone filed out.

As they walked to the truck, a man with his son quickly caught up with them. He was slight in build, with a blue and white striped suit and bow tie. "Excuse me," he addressed Babe. "My son owes your boy an apology, and I regret his words. He told me—"

Babe put two and two together after the previous night's discussion about sticking the gut punch after a rude remark. "He made a racial slur regarding my boy? I told Chris it wouldn't be the last and to get over it." The man nervously glanced at the big man's arms, and it was apparent it made him uncomfortable. "Chris needs to thicken his skin and let it roll off. All three of our boys are protective of their mom. She's Antoine Noelle's youngest daughter." The blood drained from the man's face. Yeah, not only did his kid step in a pile of shit with a Marine dad built like a warrior, but the foul doubled, if not tripled, adding that Chris' mom was the youngest offspring of the well-known powerhouse family. The Noelles were known for their business prowess, but there was also an underlying question about their connection with the Mob, and no one crossed them.

The boy reluctantly apologized; the pair bid farewell and hurried to their car. Babe imagined the boy would get a word or two from his father; it looked like the man couldn't get away fast enough, almost tripping over his own feet. *Well. That is funny. What'd he think I was going to pop him in his polished face? People!*

"That's a lesson, Chris. You never know who the person you're talking to is, so keep your thoughts to yourself; it works for me." They got in the truck homeward bound.

Chris pondered the situation the entire way home, leaning on his fist, elbow crooked against the window. "Sir, do you think I'm gonna get much taller? I know I'm gonna get more buff," and he flexed. "I've been hitting the weights a lot lately. Looking at that dorky little man, he was about to shit himself, especially when you said Trinity was a Noelle." Babe listened to Chris' non-stop thoughts as they entered the house.

Occupied with concerns about Coach Kennedy, Babe made his way into the study and shut the doors. Rocking back in the desk chair, laced hands behind his head, he formulated what to say. Hearing Coach was sick raised red flags and hurt deep down to his core. The man was always one for solid advice. Even though Babe didn't talk often, maybe to say one or two words, Coach knew what was in his heart. In the echoes of his mind, he heard Coach's words, 'You're an easy target, son. For some reason, insecure boys or ones with a point to prove will always want to challenge the big kid. Don't buy into their insecurity; you know who you are, and be comfortable with that. You hear me, Vicarelli?' He had been right. Kids in school and strangers on the street—it didn't matter; many tried to pick a fight with him. He took Coach's message under advisement and didn't engage, only to avoid being hit or kicked. He told Siri, "Call Coach."

The man sounded spry. "How the hell are you Vicarelli? I saw your beautiful bride at the boys' school a few days ago. Ernie likes your boys; he said they were well-mannered. I had to laugh and tell him they were bound to be respectful if they were yours. You didn't put up with bullshit. I imagine Ernie also told you about my condition, prompting this call. The diagnosis was shocking to me, but it was my wife who noticed the subtleties."

Babe drummed his fingers on the desk and sighed, "Mr. Fox mentioned you were ill but did not disclose anything further. This call is to find out if I can be of help to you or your wife."

The coach chuckled, "It's not sick like that, Vic. I have what they call the long goodbye, Alzheimer's. I'm only beginning the journey. Some people live a long life, maybe don't remember part of it, but others go quicker. I haven't decided which one I'd rather. Talk for another time, my friend. We can enjoy a bottle of whiskey or a few brews. Tell me about your boys. You've never given me the full skinny on them. I met them at the wedding, and they seemed like good kids."

Babe rambled for about twenty minutes, taking a moment to talk about each boy. The coach found it interesting that Babe found Chris' father, who had been a Marine, gone wayward, like so many. While talking about the boys, he continually reflected on Coach's Alzheimer's. They scheduled a date for the couples to get together over dinner at Chestnut the following week. It would allow Coach to get to know the boys while Trinity got the low-down from Coach's wife. If any two people could get information from someone, it was the Trinity and Ruthie tag team. By the end of the evening, they'd find out when she noticed the behavior change and prognosis without Babe having to talk about it with his mentor unless Jack wanted to talk about it, which he doubted, knowing the nature of the man. A week would fly by.

NO RHYME OR REASON

*L*ife could be confounding. Coach had served his country valiantly and spent the better part of his adult life molding young boys into men. Now, when it was time to relax and enjoy life with his wife, he was diagnosed with Alzheimer's. While he may have many lucid years ahead, no one could give a definitive answer. *Where are you, God?* There were a plethora of degenerates and misguided fools, yet they managed to stay healthy unless by their choice, and here, a man with the heart of a servant gets struck with this thief of an illness. Before him, the age-old question was, why do bad things happen to good people? One could query why good things happen to bad people, but the circle would go round and round like a dog chasing his tail. Trinity's favorite answer for everything is, 'God is right there with you. You are not alone in bad times and good. That's the bottom line.' *One hell of a bottom line, eh, God?*

Trinity spent most of the morning getting pampered with spa treatments, relaxed, and ready to pair up with Ruthie and prepare a feast. She pulled out all the stops. Ruthie stuffed mushrooms with crabmeat, Trinity ordered a whole filet from Langenstein's, whipped up potatoes au gratin, and a large salad filled with avocado, artichoke hearts, romaine lettuce, and red onions. Ruthie made a salad dressing surpassed by none, and they instructed Babe to pick up an assortment of desserts.

The boys joined him in the hunt for the perfect desserts, including stopping by a few local bakeries. Ruthie already had bread pudding on the go, a recipe going back generations in her family, and a taste to die for. Reg began asking questions about Coach Kennedy. Babe became exceedingly quiet. "Is something wrong, sir? You seem almost sad."

"I am sad." They made eye contact in the rearview mirror. "Coach has a terrible illness, and before you ask, no, you can't catch it. Have you heard of Alzheimer's? It's called the long goodbye because as it progresses, the brain literally shrinks, and it starts simple, like forgetting things from day to day, sometimes moment to moment, so if he asks you a question, answer him and don't act smartass if he asks it again. Better yet, when we get home, y'all look it up on your computer." Quiet enveloped the car, and what had been a constant stream of exaggerated tasting delights became solemn. Sitting in the passenger seat, Chris drummed his thumb on his leg. "What's up with you?" Babe asked.

"Nothing of importance." Was that an answer saying not now, none of your business, or honestly nothing? Chris wasn't one to talk about feelings— *I get that*, Babe concurred in his mind.

With boxes of goodies, they pulled into the driveway. Trinity came out onto the porch, her hand shading her eyes from the glare of the sun. "Good Gracious, y'all buy out Sucré?" Jake was filled with an overabundance of sugar, emitting energy and wound tight like a top. "Y'all acting like small children. Certainly, you can handle a little sugar at your age. I want your rooms straightened. It's not that I'm expecting anyone to go upstairs, but just in case. Shower and dress casually but not like slobs." They jetted upstairs, bickering the whole way. "Vic, you got them acting like sugar bitches. How many meringues and petit fours did they have?"

Babe furrowed his brows, "I don't know, I didn't count. They each had a box and picked what they wanted." He scooped her from behind as her mouth was wagging complaints. "What you need is a little sugar." He picked her up and carried her to their bedroom.

Hours later, Mays called Babe. "I have some strange news for you. Stuart and I had a long conversation about Elloise. She's dead. He said Austin called him frantic because the Baton Rouge police paid him a visit regarding the murder of Elloise Eglin. The police found her body, and some thug shot her point blank in a trailer park. He couldn't imagine why she was there, and now the police think he played a part in the crime. Get this, he asked if Stuart would be a character witness. I had thoughts circling the drain. Babe, do you know anything about the situation?" They both knew the honest answer and how it would go.

"What do you think?" he asked sarcastically. "I wouldn't waste one of my bullets on Elloise or the thug." He hadn't lied. He hadn't used one of his bullets or even his gun. He preferred hands-on, but since the place was a dive and the weapon was already in his hand, he didn't care about the mess, so he made it quick and easy. Pop. Pop. Deal done.

Silence.

"What do you think about me representing Austin if he asks?"

"Hmph," Babe groaned. "That's up to you, but I wouldn't represent the guy."

"Think about it, bro. He gave us a heads-up about the woman calling her hitman. Now, onto less heady subjects. When do y'all want to travel to Narvik?" Mays was well on his way to not thinking about the murder of Elloise.

Babe was silent for a moment, thinking. "In a month. Give Trinity a bit more time. I'll check with her and Ruthie. It may not be a good time for her. I gotta give her time off; the woman is dutiful in her responsibilities. I don't know what we'd do without her. Then there's the issue of Chris starting L.S.U. I'll check with Bjorn and then book the tickets. Y'all come in a couple of days before. Look, it's too late to call tonight; he'll already have had a snoot full. I'll call in the AM."

"Okay, Later, my brother," Mays sounded thoughtful.

Babe gave a wordier goodbye than usual, considering he generally ended with a sharp bye and disconnect.

Babe heard Trinity and Ruthie in the kitchen getting everything set for Coach Kennedy and his wife. It was the first dinner party, so to speak since they'd lived on Chestnut. Actually, Babe thought, the first he'd ever had. Trinity's parents' Sunday meal was just the family getting together. One may call it something else, but it was what it was.

The princess was in the playpen; he leaned over and picked her up. Trinity questioned who Babe had been on the phone with. "I have a question for you two ladies. Would the coast be clear for a trip to Norway in four weeks?"

Ruthie had her hand on her hip and turned to face him. "And just how long would you two be away? Now, with Chancée, the job has gotten a bit harder. Would you be willing to have my sister, Sarah, stay with me? She and I can stay in the same room." Babe had to think about it. He figured if she was Ruthie's sister, it should be okay. He acquiesced, joking, he said, no big family barbeques. The older lady rolled her eyes and shook her head commenting in a muffled voice something to the effect of 'as if.'

Babe pulled up the calendar on his phone. "We will leave Sunday, June 30, and return the fourteenth of July. Does that work for you ladies?" Trinity said they'd miss the Fourth of July extravaganza at her parents' house, but Ruthie, her sister, and the kids would be more than welcome. "I'll touch base with Bjorn tomorrow morning. Now, we all need to get dressed for our guests. C'mon, Trinity Marie," and he grabbed her hand.

Once upstairs and alone, Babe pulled her close to him, slowly removing her clothes. He bathed her body with kisses as he stepped out of his jeans, dramatically swept her into his arms, and laid her on the bed. She smiled, "You teased me before, let's make this real. We have time, so calm down, sport, and let's take this slowly and enjoy every second." He straddled her, then rolled over, pulling her on top of him. "I know what you want, and as you often say, your wish is my command, but I say, your wish is my pleasure. Vic, you gonna moan for me?" Once the fireworks were over, they showered, dressed, and put the finishing touches on the welcome for their guests. The boys sat in the den, dressed casually but nicely.

Ruthie was full of questions before Coach and his wife arrived. She'd heard bits and pieces about Babe's upbringing, but by the time Trinity finished filling in the blanks, the old gal looked at Babe with even more respect. The doorbell rang.

Trinity had forgotten how old Babe's coach was, and it took her by surprise, or had his illness aged him by a decade? His wife, coiffed with a new color in her hair, was still attractive and doted on Jack but not in an emasculating way.

From tasty teasers to a delicious dinner, Jack enthralled the boys with stories about Babe as a high schooler, and they were full of questions. Trinity had a hard time picturing her man as a boy. Her emotions swoll with sadness, happiness, and finally, contentment. Coach excused himself and went to the car. To everyone's excitement, he returned with yearbooks. Babe had forgotten what he looked like as a kid. In eighth grade, he was a foot taller than most of the boys. His beard had started coming in, and they could see a slight shadow on his face. Across part of his jawline was a vivid scar. Jacob piped in, "Sir, what is that cut on your jaw? Did you get in a fight?"

Coach quickly shut the book. Babe said, "It's okay, Jack; they know my father was an abusive bastard. Guys, remember when I told you about the last physical confrontation with the sperm donor? He received a beat down from me that disabled his shoulder, but I got a pretty good slice from a kitchen table knife before disabling him. I think that's what pushed me over the edge. It's barely visible now with my beard and fading time." He saw Trinity's eyes fill, to which he responded with a slight shake of his head. The boys expressed their opinions, which would handily fill the money jar.

"Money jar?" Jack questioned. Ruthie explained that the Marine language in the house was an offense settled with cold, hard cash. His wife piped in that maybe she would start a money jar; it would easily fund a trip anywhere. The boys disguised their laughter well amidst coughs.

Jack and Babe retired to the study for some private conversation, giving Ruthie and Trinity time to pump the information about the coach's prognosis from his wife.

Babe poured a snifter of Brandy and handed it to Jack, then sat on an adjacent chair. Coach set the glass down, cracked his knuckles, and set his jaw. "There's more to my diagnosis than my wife knows about, and she is not to know." He looked Babe directly in his eyes. He nodded in acknowledgment.

The coach explained that yes, he had Alzheimer's but also inoperable tumors in his brain, and his progression was rapid. In other words, he had little time left. Babe's eyes teared. Coach held his hand up and moved his pointer finger in a no, no, no manner. "Okay, your story to tell. You know how influential you've been in my life. I can't imagine a world without you." Babe drew in a deep sniffle and nodded, clenching his jaw.

Coach held his brandy up and said, "Here's to great memories!" Babe started asking questions about headaches, what made him suspect he was sick, and Coach shook his head no. "My big friend, this will be the last time we see each other, and I don't want to get bogged down with medical shit; I live with it. One of my best memories is of a wrestling tournament where your first opponent was a boy not as tall as you but as big as a bull. I thought you were going to get your clock cleaned. To my surprise, you detected his weakness and pinned him every time in seconds. The other coach accused us of cheating, saying you were too old. Your grandfather was there and pulled your birth certificate from his wallet. Watch what people accuse you of because, quite often, they're the ones committing the violation, and such was the case. His wrestler was over the age limit for high school competitions. The boy couldn't get a scholarship because his grades were so poor. I think he failed two or three times. After that incident, I carried a copy of your birth certificate with me whenever we had a tournament. What's your favorite memory?"

Babe sat back in the chair, rocked, and crossed his leg. Through tears, he displayed a wide smile. "That's easy. Two times come to mind immediately. You were the first person to take my side at school when those boys were tag-teaming me. Nobody else ever took my side. Hell, it happened all the time, and boom, I'd get sent to the principal's office. Eventually, the office would send me back to class, but I missed half of lunch and all of my free time. The second was on the most brilliant day of my life, marrying Trinity. You looked so sharp in your dress blues."

They talked about Babe growing up with his father; he admitted to the abuse and his shattering Gino's shoulder. Coach said he knew it had been Hell but didn't know how bad. In high school, he was mostly at his grandfather's, and while Babe loved him, it was in an old people's world, and there was no typical teenage bullshit. He recounted taking the street car to Canal Street and that there was a girl, a working girl, about his age that he'd hang with. Babe saw Moxie's pimp slap her around, so he made fast tracks to save the girl. The big kid hopped off the streetcar and sprinted to the melee. Not bragging, he admitted to breaking the guy's jaw. Moxie and Babe hung out all day, and when it started to get dark, Babe brought her to Chestnut with him and let her stay in one of the guest rooms. The arrangement worked for a week, but the housekeeper discovered her and reported it to his grandfather, Rune. His grandfather was fantastic and helped her find a place besides his home. It was a house full of runaway teenage girls. Then came the talk about the birds and bees. Coach and Babe laughed when he said the boat had long sailed by that time.

Trinity knocked on the door, "Hey, y'all, you've gossiped long enough. It's like a freakin' eighth-grade party where the boys stand on one side and the girls on the other. Man up, Vicarelli." Jack chuckled at her remark.

Returning to the living room, Coach regaled stories of Babe and his extraordinary talents. He said all the coaches wanted him and that he would have made an outstanding athlete no matter the sport. Trinity had her turn to tell Jack about Babe's descriptions of Jack Kennedy, his hero. The boys came down for a second helping of bread pudding, which provided an opportunity to visit with the big guy's friend. It was a relaxing evening. Ruthie speculated the money jar had reached a hundred dollars in that one night. They made memories for a lifetime.

There was a heavy cloud cover, so the moon wasn't bright; it was merely a wispy, dim glow in the sky. Passing by a shop window, Jude Baham checked his reflection, and no matter how hard he tried, he couldn't understand what made him a chic magnet. He was swoon-worthy, his mother said; girls had flocked to him since he was a kid. The fairer sex would say that he looked like a younger version of Johnny Depp, sexy and suave in a bad-boy kind of way. His dark hair pulled into a man-bun, set off his coal-colored eyes. Girls had called them hypnotic and mysterious, but as far as he was concerned, he was like any ordinary guy.

In the reflection, he saw a girl scoping him out. She was hot with waist-length blonde waves, perfect doe-like eyes, and a body with curves in all the right places. He turned, they made eye contact, and she smiled. She seductively bit one side of her plump lower lip. Was she sending out signals? What harm could it do to offer to buy her a drink? The worst that could happen was she'd say no.

"Wanna grab a drink; you look lonely standing here all alone." The vibes she was putting out didn't shout hooker, just a beautiful lonely girl. She twirled her hair around her finger and bashfully looked through her bangs. She seemed scared and, understandably, being propositioned by a stranger. "My name is Jude. What's your name?"

"Heather," she whispered. "Yeah, I'll go for a drink. Where?" She shuffled from foot to foot, obviously nervous.

"Maybe a hotel lounge, like at the Sonesta, where there are lotsa people." He was trying to calm her nerves. She was pretty and didn't come across as cheap. Whether it developed into anything else didn't matter. He hadn't gone out to get laid; he got out because living alone after being raised in a house with four sisters was boring. He had a studio apartment on Esplanade, down the street from the law firm where he worked as a paralegal while attending Tulane Law School.

"I guess that'd be good. I'm sure you hear it all the time—you look like the movie star Johnny Depp. You really do." He had to attentively listen as she spoke softly, a little more than a whisper. "Jude, that's a cool name." She giggled. "What do you do?"

"I'm a paralegal by day and a law student by night, usually. I took a break tonight after class. What do you do?" It was as if she hid behind her hair, so timid and shy.

She blushed, "You're not gonna believe this, but I work in the Loyola library. We're almost neighbors." The stars seemed to align, and this sweet beauty had potential as a girlfriend. It'd been a year since his last relationship, which ended in disaster. His ex broke his heart. Jude thought they'd get married after he graduated. When he professed his love, she sliced him to the quick, saying he provided her with eye candy and a stiff dick. His closest sister, Rachel, called the girl a skank and told him he was better off without her. He felt a slight tug in his heart, remembering the hurt he felt when she spoke so boldly.

"No kidding?" he asked reflectively.

Their connection seemed strong. Dare he invite her to his place? It was as though they were on the same wavelength because she asked where he lived. She lived uptown, she said, so his place was a far cheaper taxi ride. They could have hoofed it, but one never knew what could lie ahead on the city's streets.

Heather held his hand on the ride to his place. When he looked closer at her by the light of the cab, it shocked him; she was much older than seemed in the dark. It wasn't a deal breaker, but not a happy surprise. He had thought they were both in their late twenties or early thirties like him, but she was clearly forty-plus. He paid the driver, unlocked the door, and led the way to his loft.

Once inside, he barely had time to get his thoughts together when she was all over him. She kissed him deeply and tugged at his belt. It wasn't what he had envisioned—no soft petting and delicate kisses; no, she was passionate as though starved for male attention. He whispered against her neck, "Slow down, let's take our time." Apparently, those were not the words she wanted to hear. She pulled away as though soul-crushed. "Don't be upset, Heather; I wanted you to enjoy yourself. Whatever floats your boat." She liked that answer and proceeded to pull her top off, release her bra, and drop her skirt, revealing her nakedness. He dropped his pants and pulled his shirt over his head.

Jude gave her what she wanted with a hard ride. She gave him detail by detail what she wanted. While this barbarian sexploit was a first, he found himself getting into it and letting go of any inhibitions he had. It was an opportunity to try everything he had always wanted to experience, and the more primal he was, the more she got off. The neighbor banged on the door. "Jude, you're waking everyone up. Slow your game."

Heather jumped out of the bed and opened the door. She was stark naked. "Wanna join the party?" The neighbor freaked, turned, and went back into his apartment. Turning around, she saw Jude wrapped in a towel, his mouth agape. "A bug is going to fly into your mouth if you don't shut it," and she laughed. "I'm getting in the bath." He had no words to express his bewilderment, so he crawled back into his bed and dozed off. What seemed like hours later, he woke to her straddling him. Even though he was bleary-eyed, there was no mistaking the chef's knife in her hand as she proceeded to plunge it into his chest over and over.

A DEADLY STREAK

*M*ax shot a rubber band at Trey. "Hey, Sledgehammer, what is your problem? You're supposed to be a grown-ass man, but you act like a kid." Ping, another rubber band hit Trey in the chest. "Dude?"

Max had a shit-eating grin with a devilish twinkle in his eyes. "I met someone, a cute redhead, probably early forties. Nice, lady. She was at Mother's when I picked up my poboy. She works on Gravier as some kind of personal assistant and was picking up her boss' lunch. She picks it up every day; the guy must be a rotundo. She asked for my number," he double-lifted his brows. Trey couldn't help but laugh inside; Max had no room to call anybody out for being hefty; he sported a round gut, himself.

Trey was looking over a report and casually asked, "She give you hers?"

Max rocked in his chair, "You gotta rain on my parade, Kimble? I ain't got her number yet, but I will get it. She's my type, real chatty. I got her life story waiting in line; you know how long the line is at Mother's. No kids, never been married, not into Yoga or jogging, and likes, get this, Real Crime drama. Bet your ass I didn't tell her I was a cop, at least not yet."

Trey's and Max' cells chimed simultaneously—murder on Esplanade.

Babe breathed heavily on Trinity's neck, which made her giggle and squirm. As much as she struggled to get away, he had her pinned and diligently pursued the tickling. "Boy, if you think you're gonna seduce me—" and she broke out in hysterical laughter. "Stop; you gave me goosebumps and are making the hair grow on my legs." She squealed again.

"Shh, Trinity, the baby," he laughed.

"Dammit, Babe, you wake her up with your foolishness, and she's all yours." He rolled off of her. "Tell me about Narvik and what we're gonna do when we get there." He grabbed his phone from the nightstand, googled Norway, specifically Narvik, and scrolled through the limited photos.

She curled against his body. He kissed the top of her head and pulled her on top of him. "I just wanted to look at you. It looks like you are starting to fill out again. I don't know how to put this because whatever I say, you'll spin it the wrong way. You no longer look sickly. Chris was right about the boys in his class; I bet they all looked at you with lustful thoughts."

They made use of the time Chancée slept. Like almost all things, time was a healer, and the more time they spent together, the closer their bond. Travel plans developed, and Trinity was eager to meet Babe's Uncle Bjorn and enjoy the cooler temperatures. The fifties and sixties in late June and early July would be a welcomed relief from NOLA's nineties, but it felt like a hundred. Trinity started planning her wardrobe for the trip. Leaving the last week of June and returning at the beginning of the third week in July was ideal; they'd only miss the Fourth of July festivities.

It was not far off, so Trinity began to shop and pack while surfing the web to discover points of interest in Norway. After a Zoom call between Mays and Lark, Trinity already felt like she'd made a friend with Mays' girlfriend. Time was going to pass quickly.

Mark Clemmons, newly graduated from the University of North Carolina, met with some of his previous high school buddies at Pat O'Brien's. It had been a helluva night. They were all pretty trashed. Sitting at a table next to theirs was a brunette with shoulder-length hair. She kept checking her watch and looking toward the entrance. She'd get up, walk to the entrance, wait five minutes, and return to her table. The disappointment on her face spelled it out—somebody had stood her up.

They had a rowdy crowd at their table. What harm could come from adding another pretty face to their group? Mark introduced himself and invited her to their party of friends. It had to sting sitting at a table by herself with boisterous drunks at the next table. Everybody was getting pretty intoxicated. The girl was quiet, and he could tell she felt awkward. "What's your name?" he asked.

Quietly, she answered, "Ann."

"Pam?"

"No, Ann," she spoke louder. "I'm sorry it's just, um, so loud." She was obviously shy. Mark introduced her to his friends and some of the girls crowded around the table. They smiled at her one by one, but she could see them checking her out and rolling their eyes. He felt for her.

He leaned into her, "Want to go somewhere else? My friends are not usually such assholes. They're all pretty drunk."

She looked downward. "I think I'm gonna go home, well, back to the hotel. Thanks."

"I just met you; gimme a chance I can be a fun guy." He slung a cheesy, toothy smile her way and raised an eyebrow. "Too bad I don't have my Groucho Marx glasses; they always get a smile." She smiled at his playfulness. "I know, how about we go to Café du Monde? I could use some coffee about right now."

She giggled. "Okay, I guess."

Mark told his friends he was leaving and led the way out. Ann was painfully shy, and getting her to talk was like pulling teeth. He hoped once she relaxed, she'd be more chatty. With each passing block, she began to open up. She was from Gulfport and was in town for a nursing conference. She was cute, not hot or sexy, but cute. He could see how she'd be a nurse, being so sweet. One of the guys from the conference had asked her to meet him at Pat O's at ten thirty. They had an early morning seminar, so they hadn't planned on a long night out. Mark felt sorry for her but imagined she'd confront the douche in the morning class.

Ann ended up being a talker, after all. With a couple of orders of beignets and coffee, she was ready to cab it back to her hotel. For some reason, he felt responsible for ensuring she got to the hotel. They grabbed a cab and headed to her hotel on Convention Center Boulevard.

The cab pulled up to the hotel. Ann quietly asked, "Do you want to come up? If not, I totally understand. I mean, I took you from your friends; you probably want to get back to them."

Mark leaned forward, paid the cab fare, and answered, "Sure." He wasn't certain where the interaction would land, but thought, what the hell, why not?

Riding up in the elevator, she kept her head looking down like she was ashamed. "I don't usually act so forward. You probably think—"

"Heck no," he quipped, "I don't think anything." He followed behind her when they exited the elevator and then into her room. The only lighting was a dim corner lamp. When the door closed, she spun to face him, giving him a hard, deep kiss. She started to undo his jeans, grabbed his junk, then turned away and headed to the bed. She pulled a wrapper from the drawer and rolled the condom onto him. Her clothes were off in seconds, and she was hot and ready for him. The night was turning into something he would have never imagined. She was skillful in the sack, better than anyone he'd ever been with, especially for such a sweet girl. Vixen was the thought that came to mind.

She demanded more and more, kinkier than he'd ever been. It was apparent that it wasn't her first rodeo, which made him think of a tee shirt he once saw at the beach, Call a Nurse They Got Bedside Manner. At this juncture, he'd agree wholeheartedly. She jumped out of bed, went into the bathroom, flushed the toilet, and came out quickly. She mounted him, grinding down hard on him, and then, out of nowhere, she plunged a knife deep into his chest, wildly hatcheting it over and over. Although dead, his eyes still registered the shock and horror.

The woman jumped in the shower, washed the blood off her, and wiped the room down, leaving no evidence. As she primped her short red hair, she reflected on Memphis. The cops started to get close after her ninth slaughter. She chuckled when she thought about Dwayne; she dated the guy until he revealed himself for who he was. It was kill or be killed. He tried, but her tactical skills made her fearless. Moving to Louisiana was a good solution to avoiding discovery. New Orleans was easy; the people were outgoing, setting themselves up for whatever might come their way.

Had it not been for the wild attack on her, Pandora's box would've stayed closed and her propensity latent. Her insatiable desires would have remained locked up forever. Whether it came from deep-rooted anger over her mother's boyfriend shtupping her younger step-sister or perhaps the ugly comments boys called her growing up. So what? She was an athlete and muscular, which had no bearing on her sexuality. There wasn't a lesbian bone in her body, not that she had anything against them; everyone deserved to answer their sexual yearnings. The question remained: how much longer would her mother's credit card work? Eventually, she would have to settle and accept her authentic identity and keep her penchant for brutality well hidden. She'd keep the spree until they declined the credit card.

A week passed, and Max would go to Mother's at a different time each day, hoping to run into his red-haired crush. For the most part, he preferred longer hair, but the short pixie look was perfect for her. He talked to Trey incessantly about the woman. Trey hadn't seen him so enamored since wife number two. Even some of the other detectives watched as his waistline reduced slowly, and he had a pep in his step with newfound energy from working out. Even his attire looked freshened up.

The chick was a warranted distraction from the heinous murders that plagued the city. They had another slasher on their hands; young men were dropping like flies, dying in blood-saturated beds with chests that resembled minced meat. The killer left no evidence.

Max grabbed his keys. "Padna, I'm going to take a spin around to see if anything looks hinky out there." The presumption was the sicko targeted gay men. The amount of rage displayed with the mutilated bodies; they leaned in a male-on-male connection.

Turning onto Poydras Street, he slowly passed Mother's and checked the line out. Bingo! He parked, put his NOPD permit on the dashboard, and rushed to get in line. She spotted him, smiled, and approached him, giving up her spot in the queue. She had a childish giggle, "Hi, Max. I wondered if I'd see you again. How can you lose weight eating here? I gain five pounds just looking at the poboys. New tie?" He didn't say yes, although everyone in the department complimented the new ties and shirts.

The line moved forward, and his phone rang. He ignored the call, something he never did. Max continued to be as charming as possible. "I was hoping you'd call me. I'd like to take you to dinner and not Mother's," he chortled. For the first time, she noticed his shield at his waist. Instead of dodging the situation, she enthusiastically accepted the challenge. "By the way, my name is Gwen Peters. Give me your phone." She tapped in her contact information. "Now you have my digits. Call me; maybe we can meet at Oceana or Muriel's."

He shifted his feet. "I'm in the Quawdda most of the time cuz of work. Ya like Mandina's? It's in Mid-City."

"Sure. It's close to my place." She switched her bag from one shoulder to the other. She'd strained her right arm from the last murderous event. She told the truth: Gwen lived in Mid-City in half a double on Banks with her grandmother. "We can meet Thursday night, say eight? Where do you live?"

He shook his head, "Ain't no restaurant near my house dat I'm taking you to. I'm in Gentilly. I have a small yellow brick two bedroom, one bath ranch style. It's the same house everyone built in the fifties with a front picha winda. My uncle, bless his soul, willed it to me. Like me, he had no children, and I joined the force because of him. Some piece of shit shot him while he was on the job. S'cuse my French, but it's true. Shot him in the back. Coward." She couldn't agree more; her conquests were always face-to-face.

The line had moved up to the entrance of the building. "Sounds like a date, Max Sledge. Thursday at eight, see you at Mandina's." She smiled with fluttery lashes.

"I'll see ya then, Gwen," Max flirted.

She disappeared into the restaurant while Max returned to his unit. He called Trey back. "Sorry, I was detained."

"Oh, yeah? What's her name?" he busted his chops. "We got another one, dude. Poor kid just graduated from college. The M.E. found a receipt from Pat O's. He was there last night. Maid found him, bro. It's a mess. The kid was so joe-college, you could just tell. I don't think the dude was gay, dunno why I say that, but the hotel remembers he came in with a brunette college co-ed." Max could hear the pen clickety-clicking away. Trey was all in on the investigation. "Hey, I looked in the database to see if there were similar reports from other cities and snap, Memphis had nine identical ones. They had the same thinking we did at first about the murderer being male, but they soon came to suspect the doer was female. For the most part, I always think, single white male, but we maybe got a fucking Aileen Wuornos, bud."

"Gwenny, that you, sugar?" Her grandmother entered the living area. "You been gone awhile; I was getting worried about you. How'd the job interview go? Getting a teaching job used to be easy, but now, it seems like they're cutting back. Maybe you should have stayed in Memphis, sweetheart. I love having you here, but you might have to take a job that's not in teaching. That's what the neighbors said." The older gal went back into the kitchen to stir a pot. "Oh, Jimmy from Memphis called and asked for you to call him back. Gwenny, you oughta give him a chance; you're not gettin' any younger."

Skipping over the details Jimmy had called was her way of saying there was no way in Hell. They had history, which wasn't pretty; besides, he was in Memphis and too old for her taste. "The interview I had today was for a position as a personal assistant. It pays the same as a teacher, minus the benefits, which sucks, but at least it's a job, right?" She spoke as she left the room.

Once inside her room, she pulled the wig out of her bag and opened the closet, where she had fifteen other wigs in every color imaginable. She had each carefully pinned to a Styrofoam mannequin head. She took off her clothes and stood before the mirror, examining her body. Even after entering her forties, she still had well-defined muscles and a great body.

Gwen reflected. After graduating from high school at eighteen, she was military-bound. The Army recruiter was particularly excited when Gwen accepted his spiel and applied. She was the easiest sell. Uncle Sam would pay for her education; it was a chance to see the world. They promised to train her in a multitude of different jobs that would parlay into a position in the civilian world. In her sleeveless sundress, her perfectly defined arms were impressive. The Army jumped at having a recruit so physically fit.

Boot camp had been challenging, but she figured she wouldn't stand out as an oddball. Most of the ladies were fearless like she was and athletic, not a freak. It didn't bother her that a couple of the women hit on her. If anything, it was a compliment, not an insult, even though it wasn't her slant.

Gwen made it through Boot Camp, but her superiors had dressed her down for her anger issues on a few occasions. Enough so that after two years of service, the ranking officers discharged her as psychologically unfit to serve. It was just another tick on her belt of failures. To her, it was the height of insult.

One Saturday night, months after returning from the Army, she decided to let her anger go, accept that she wasn't in the military, and move on. She'd already started college, *so much for being on Uncle Sam's dime*, she thought. She drove around Memphis and landed at a Country Western bar. There were more boots and cowboy hats than you could shake a stick at. The band was good, but her fascination came from watching people ride the mechanical bull. The internal debate began: should she try it or not? Quite a few people landed on their ass, so it wouldn't be like she would be the lone ranger.

The man working the bull was about her age, maybe a couple of years older. He had shaggy, sandy blond hair, hazel eyes, and a body that wouldn't quit. When a guest wasn't riding or trying to ride the bull, he would tease as he rode the mechanical beast, ramping it up with suggestive maneuvers. He lit a flame of desire inside of her. She got in line; stomach twitters over a stranger were new, and she liked it. The reaction created a warmth between her legs, almost taking her breath away. It wasn't like she was a virgin, but after being crushed by the love of her life, she wasn't quick to bed anyone. She hadn't been around the block, as some would say.

It was her turn. "Hey, darlin', have you ridden before?" She shook her head no. His smile beamed, "Well then, you are going to have the time of your life. It will probably take several times before you get the knack." He explained what to do. The challenge began. She was a natural. She gripped the bull with her thighs rather than let her legs flail like other riders before her. A crowd drew close as she mastered the ride amid whistles and cheers. When it stopped, the handsome cowpoke had a gleam in his eyes. "Little lady, you sure you never done this before?"

"Nope. I guess I did good?" Gwen coyly smiled.

"I'd say. How about getting a drink with me when I go on break?" He literally had a hat in hand.

"Sure. What's your name other than Bull Master? I'm Gwen." She turned her toes inward, standing on the sides of her feet. She'd rocked in that position whenever she was nervous since she was a child.

"D-wayne," he answered in a slow Southern drawl with a dimpled smile. "Dwayne Shelby, my family owns this bar and a couple more in town. Wait at the bar and tell Chuck, the big bartender, to put your drink on my tab." Being in school at the University of Memphis, living with her mother's sister and on-again-off-again husband, she could save a few pennies, but having someone buy her drinks was even more economical.

She sat on a barstool and grabbed a handful of peanuts, waiting for Chuck. The more than husky bartender didn't take long to take her order. When she said Dwayne had said to put it on his tab, the barkeep grinned knowingly. Was the joke on her? "Give me an empty glass and pour the Jack in front of me. He took on a look of concern as his brows furrowed and the gleeful in-the-know smile dissipated.

Chuck did as asked but inquired confusedly, "What was all that about, if you don't mind me asking, ma'am?"

She ran her finger around the rim of the glass. "I saw you grin, and I thought there might be some shenanigans, like a roofie."

The shock and disbelief on his face indicated such was not the case.

The man stammered, "Uh, um, no ma'am. If it's cuz I smiled, it's just Dwayne hasn't had an interest in anyone since Tammy Sue up and left town without so much as a word. She broke his heart. Roofie? No ma'am. Dwayne don't need no drug to capture the attention of a lady. All the girls in town were happy when Tammy Sue left. They figured they'd get their chance." Her shoulders drew up toward her ears, and her back hunched slightly, indicating embarrassment as her lips turned downward. "Dwayne has another fifteen minutes til he breaks. You need some fresh peanuts? Ya know ones every Tom, Dick, or Harry ain't put their paws in." She shook her head no.

It felt like Dwayne cut his time with the bull short as he pulled up the barstool beside her and ordered a Coke. Conversation came easy with the handsome stud. After a drink and a long fact-finding adventure, Gwen said she had to leave, explaining she lived with her aunt. He asked for her phone number, took her phone, and added his name to her contact list. He told her he was off Monday through Wednesday and only worked twelve to five on Sunday, then asked if she would like to catch a movie or go to dinner with him.

Her stomach had a ballet of butterflies, making her words barely audible. "Yes, I would. Which night?" She was somewhat bashful, probably because the guy was so damn hot, but offered her address. He walked her to her car and said he'd see her Monday night. He knew right where her aunt's place was, which surprised her. The spark returned in her belly. He took her hand and kissed the top of it. That's how it all began, she reminisced.

The one date parlayed into a hot, heavy romance, and she moved in with him. Dwayne had a beautiful home. They had a fourteen-year happily ever-after relationship, and it was still going strong. She stayed in school most of the time, changing from one major to another, and eventually, at thirty-four, she had twelve more hours to graduate. She worked at the bar, sometimes riding the bull. Men seemed to like watching her. Much as his family and her family wanted them to marry, neither had the desire for marriage and definitely no children. Their life was bliss.

One night, he came home from work cloaked with the strong scent of a woman's perfume. They rarely argued, but this time, it got heated because he was drunk, she thought. He called her awful names; she stormed into their bedroom to get her shoes and was readying to walk out. "Gwen, I'm warning you. No one walks away from me and stays healthy. Now you settle down, and we can make up."

She turned to face him, "You think for one second I'm gonna sleep with you? Think again." She had strapped one shoe tightly and attempted to strap the other when he picked her up, threw her on the bed, and began ripping her clothes off of her. Gwen kicked him in the gut, which made him land on his ass.

"I warned you." He pulled a switchblade out of his front pocket. He came at her. Instinct took over; she side-stepped the knife and knocked it from his grasp. She scrambled for the blade and shoved it into his gut just under his ribs. Knowing how powerful his family was in Memphis, she had to make it unquestionable that it was self-defense. She slid the blade from under her earlobe to her chin, careful not to nick the carotid and a few nicks on her arms and hands. That wasn't enough; she threw her body against the door jamb, making contact with her cheek. In minutes, it began to swell. Grabbing her cell, she dialed nine-one-one. In a frantic, emotional, put-on wrecked voice, she hysterically began crying, saying her boyfriend had attacked her.

"I fought him off, and his knife ended up in his stomach. He needs help, or he'll die. He was drunk; he didn't mean it." With a calm voice, the dispatch told her the police were on the way. She'd stay on the phone with her until they arrived. Ten minutes tops, they pulled up. Before they could knock, she threw open the door. The blood down the front of her and her torn clothes certainly set a dismal scene for the boyfriend.

One of the officers stayed with her, and the other went to the boyfriend. "Oh, shit, McNeil, it's Seth Shelby's boy." The sound of the crash truck echoed in the late-night air. The paramedics jumped into action.

"Girl, you are so lucky; one more inch, you would have bled out like that," the paramedic snapped her fingers. "For sure, you're going to have a shiner, and the ER doc will need to put in a couple of stitches." The EMT was a forceful mid-forties who wore her hair short-styled like a man's.

"I don't feel so lucky. Dwayne just had too much to drink; he's typically not like that. He's never hit me before or anything. We've been together for almost fifteen years." The paramedic told her to be quiet and take some deep breaths.

The sound of heavy truck tires squealed into the driveway. Seth Shelby, Dwayne's father, was a sizeable man with a take-charge attitude. "Darlin', I'm sorry Dwayne treated you like that; y'all been together for a time, and he's never done like this before?" He asked. She shook her head and said no. "We will do whatever we can to make it right." Then he looked at the EMT tending to Dwayne, "And, my boy?" The medic shook his head with glassy eyes. The man walked over and looked down at his dead son. "It was bound to happen one day; his momma and I both knew it. Sweet girl," he looked at Gwen, "He was a good man; alcohol changed him. As a teenager and young man, he couldn't hold his whiskey and would fight. We were happy as could be when he stopped drinking. We seen this coming eventually; he was a terrible drunk," the man sniffled a few times. The police pulled up and entered the scene. Seth Shelby nodded to the officer with a raise of his chin. "He's dead this time, not like—" the man shut his mouth. *Like when?* She thought. *Was he pathologic and had killed his previous girlfriend, that's why she up and disappeared?* The EMTs lifted her onto a gurney, and the next thing she knew, they were flying down the interstate to the hospital.

Once at the hospital, they called her aunt, who started wailing. "I cain't believe this; Dwayne seemed like a good fella from such a well-respected family. I'm on my way." A police officer entered the emergency room where Gwen was; he needed all the facts. She repeated the story exactly like she had the dispatch. While Gwen didn't set out to kill him, it felt electrifying, like a drug. She wanted that buzz again. It would take a few weeks, a month, maybe two, for her injuries to heal, but after that, she'd wait for another man too full of himself to be leery of her. It felt like she wanted every cheating man to pay.

Her aunt came frantically through the door and, after taking one look at her, became hysterical. Seth Shelby, too, went to the ER.

Holding his hat against his chest, he humbled himself to her aunt and uncle. For such a man of importance, giving them the time of day impressed them. Once again, he offered anything to make it right. *Cha-ching!* She saw the greed in her aunt's eyes. She replied with a downcast look that Gwen might need plastic surgery, and they couldn't afford it. Mr. Shelby said he'd give them the money, and once again, he regretted his son's actions. The aunt, in turn, was sorrowful that the boy had died. Stating he was too young to die and had always been a polite, well-mannered young man. The awful night finally came to a conclusion when the hospital discharged Gwen to the care of her relatives, and they left for home.

Days and weeks passed when a check arrived in the mail. The swelling and bruising were mostly gone, and the cut under her jawline was only visible to someone up close and personal. A touch of makeup could hide it handily. Mr. Shelby was good on his word; the check was for twenty-five thousand dollars. Her aunt had figured out ten ways to spend the money in minutes, but none included her. She thought, *Fuck that!*

The uncle returned home; she guessed he heard about the check arriving. Gwen stewed as they excitedly made plans for the money. She plotted revenge on them. Gwen slowly added a tablespoon a day of a small turpentine mixture she concocted from her uncle's garage to their coffee pot. Both drank coffee all day, whereas everyone who knew Gwen knew she was into herbal tea, health food, and exercise.

She made it a point to run into one of the officers from the night of crazy. It didn't take long for them to become an item, and he admired her healthy living and enthusiasm for physical fitness. The routine of adding the lethal substance continued for a few months. While both of them suffered from indigestion and intense heartburn, Gwen would say in the presence of others that they needed to get on a healthier diet, and the amount of coffee they drank had to be the cause of their distress. Like everyone else, they poo-pooed her advice.

The afternoon came when she entered the house to find her aunt dead. She had blood around her mouth and sprayed on the cabinets. She deduced she must have been coughing up blood vigorously. Gwen quickly called her officer beau. He called it in and headed to her rescue. Heavy sobs made her inarticulate, and she had body spasms from crying so hard. The paramedics made it to her in five minutes or less. They found her uncle in the garage, crushed under his car. They presumed he had a faulty jack, and maybe it was. It had seemed like forever for the aunt to die; the accident with her uncle was kismet. Gwen put on the performance of her life as the distraught niece. It was her good fortune that they hadn't spent the twenty-five grand, had no children, and her only relative was Gwen's mother and step-sister, who did not need the house, so it became Gwen's. No one questioned her reason for wanting to sell the house; it had been traumatic for her, and most assumed it was because of the deaths.

In packing and cleaning, Gwen found an assortment of wigs in her aunt's closet, which hatched a twist to plans. Standing in front of the mirror with shoulder-length black hair birthed a new identity and a twisted ideology. She had zero remorse over the death of her aunt, and Dwayne truly was in self-defense. She could easily be the strange lady with a sad story. Even though Memphis was a big city, news spread like a small town.

People would gawk at her, whispering while others gazed at her, their eyes saddened and teary. She was either a source of gossip or a story of woe. It made no difference to her; the spree was about to begin.

RED IS THE COLOR OF THE NIGHT

*T*he name changes coincided with the wigs. One night, she'd wear a long, curly blonde wig, a gingham check shirt with pearl snaps tucked into her skin-tight denims, boots, and a western-style hat. With a padded push-up bra, the peek at the top of her blouse showed more bosom than was there. Her name for the outfit was Becky Brown from Nashville. She looked the part. In a different section of town was Funky Western Whiskey and Bar-B-Que, with a mix of African American and white men, for the most part. Leo was a short, slight, dark-skinned man who could out-dance anyone on the floor.

One look at the long-flowing blonde hair intrigued him. Disguised as Becky, Gwen took to the dancefloor despite not having a dance partner. "Hey, baby," Leo called to her, "Wanna partner, or you just want to do your own thing, in which case I'd like to watch?"

"No, darlin, I have no man to dance with." The man's face lit up, and the two danced for hours. Their bodies sometimes moving as one. "You sure can dance, Leo. You have a wife or a girlfriend?" The body language screamed yes, but he denied it. The atmosphere had gotten stuffy with the smell of perspiration and a dense overhead layer of cigarette smoke. "I'm going out for fresh air, but I'll be right back," she winked at him.

He insisted on escorting her outside. Mid-conversation, he kissed her. She pretended to be shy, but he said the way she danced, he could tell she wanted more and took her hand, pressing it against his crotch. The two kissed and petted for the next twenty minutes. Leo said he and some of his friends had a secret love nest; would she be interested? She hesitantly agreed but said she needed her car and would follow him.

The love nest was a trailer but more like a camper. They got the small digs bouncing from side to side. Once done, she ran outside to pee and returned to him, passed out in the bed and that was all she wrote. There was no time for him to react as she had stabbed him with three quick, deep jabs. His blood flowed out like water from a busted dam. Gwen quickly cleaned up, bringing anything she touched with her and wiping everything else down. She took off in her car for home. Part of her felt bad because he seemed like a nice man, but you get what you get when you cheat, and clearly, he was stepping out on his woman.

Every few nights, she'd envelope herself with a new identity. She created Chiffon from Georgia. She had dirty blonde hair with long layers of springy flips and conservative togs. Foster Newman, a traveling businessman, was the next in line. He stayed at The Peabody and had more money than sense. She enjoyed his company for a few days, but like all her male friends, he ended up with a splayed chest and a bed full of blood. She wiped everything clean and removed the dirty blonde wig, shoving it in her fake Gucci bag. Knowing there were cameras everywhere, she exited inconspicuously but quickly.

Her favorite persona was Victoria, a woman with a jet-black bob, heavy eye makeup, and dressed in all black. She called it her goth look. It was the perfect look to pick up an artist or college professor. Bainbridge Flowers was victim six. He was the only one to try and fight back, to no avail. She was lightning-fast with her weapon. The intense sexual encounter weakened the man and slowed his reaction time. Her orgasm was directly related to the butchering; the crazy sex was her seeing how far she could expand her limits. Nothing was out of bounds; consequently, some of her prey fell asleep following their landing in the realm of euphoria.

Professor Flowers had the most complex derangement. He told her to sit on his desk in his office while he knelt on the floor, lapping her as a dog drinking water, all the while calling her Mommy. He called himself the naughty boy who needed punishment. Proudly displayed on his desk was a marble swan with its head tucked beneath its wings. He engaged it in every orifice of her body, asking if he was being a good boy. That was the strangest encounter she'd ever had, and she was delighted when their encounter concluded. She stripped off her wig and used make-up wipes to remove the dramatic, heavily lined eyes. Everything fit perfectly in her backpack.

Victim Seven was a student at the local vo-tech. The boy had a foul mouth and more attitude than met his appearance. He was lower class, held himself poorly, and made himself known to her by acting obscenely— grabbing his junk, humping his friend like a dog, and burping the alphabet, all to garner the attention of Sarah Hudgins, the girl with the waist-length light brown braids and University of Tennessee Knoxville ball cap. The shadow from the cap disguised any appearance of her eyes. Her oversized hoodie and baggy jeans gave her a college kid look.

The little hip-hop-looking chick with the UT Knoxville cap liked to hang out at a local coffee shop connected to a gas station. That's where Gwen encountered low-class Willie Barnes, a grease monkey wannabe. Putting him down would be a gracious act for the rest of humanity.

The absolute reason for leaving Memphis was a close call with the police. Strutting her stuff with the rest of the working girls, Gwen had the routine down-pat. On the street, she called herself Honey. Sometimes, it was good to have the money, and she'd let the john go, but the last and final time was with Harold, a frequent flyer. In his mid-fifties, the man was sick of his wife and went into excruciating detail about her frigidity. He was the kind that liked to narrate the conquest. She explained on multiple occasions that she wasn't a conquest but bought and paid for by the hour. He pissed her off. Harold forced her into an alley, whipped out his stiffy, and started detailing what she should do. Money first, she told him, went to tuck it in the top of her shiny silver boot but came out with her blade cutting off his manhood. He screamed, bent forward, and Gwen, a.k.a. Honey, plunged the knife into the side of his neck. The screech of sirens filled the air; someone had reported the scream for help, and she evaded the police for what she felt was the last time. The police were mere minutes from catching her.

If caught, after obtaining a search warrant for her place, they'd find all the evidence they needed to bring her to justice. Part of the zeal was the excitement evading the police—the old cat-and-mouse clever game.

The papers and television news reported night after night the tale of the string of dead men, the chief, James Campbell, promising to catch the person or people involved. She had known Jimmy from adolescence when he stripped her of her innocence. He was over twenty, and she was but fourteen. Like many first loves, it didn't last; he traded her for a position with the police department. The odd thing was that Jimmy would occasionally run into Gwen, and one thing would lead to another. He hit on her relentlessly but was getting too old for her liking. All his attempts got shot down. The last night she saw Jimmy, he trapped her exiting the ladies' room. "I know who you are and what you do, and it's just a matter of time before I catch you soliciting. I'd be a good friend to have." He blocked the way, stopping her from passing, but she lucked out when another woman made him move so she could get to the restroom. Gwen hauled ass out of there. She'd have to be more on top of her game. He had no idea of her penchant. Hooking gave her spare money.

One of the ladies of the evening, not knowing Honey was the serial killer from the news, told her about New Orleans and how the cops didn't harass working girls and pretty much let them do their thing with a sexual favor now and then. It was part of the job.

Thus, she landed in New Orleans to live with her grandmother. She'd have to get a real job and fit her desires in between. Gwen merged into the scene without any suspicions or even notice.

The flight to Norway gave them time to talk, share stories, and cozy up as though they were connected forever. Trinity and Lark, Mays' squeeze, became close as though they'd known each other for years, and the girl held onto every story Trinity told. They were all reveling in the fun of a big family. Lark was enchanted. The Texas girl was fun, outspoken, and fit into their lives like a hand-to-glove. Mays and Lark had more in common than his ex, and it was a bold contrast to Babe's or Trinity's upbringing. Babe thought maybe his brother had found the love of his life.

The journey was long, and while they napped on the airplane, it was hardly a relaxing rest, except for Babe. "Big man, when I think of all the places you've flown, the miles and miles across the globe, I wonder, how could you sleep or function? I can't even sleep in these luxury seats." He chuckled at her comment. True, there had been rough military flights without the creature comforts like a bathroom.

"You get used to it, and you better sleep when you have a minute, or you'll wish you had. The fun began once on the ground, whether by landing or parachute. We had to maximize our time, constantly on high alert, like our senses were on overtime." He had a faraway trance to his appearance. Trinity shook him. "What? I was thinking how much I missed the Princess. Trinity, just because I'm quiet doesn't always mean I'm having an episode; in fact, they are becoming less and less. I think Chancée chases the demons away."

Mays wanted to hear all about Bjorn or what Babe could remember. What he remembered might fill a thimble. The one thing that stuck out to Babe was Bjorn had a red nose, which, as a kid, he was most curious about, but as an adult, he got it. The old guy was a boozer and had been for many years and, from Far's opinion, exceptionally randy with the lassies. Babe reported that their uncle also had a woman living with him. Her name was Ilsa. The old guy was entertaining, to say the least. Physically, he was their size and had a head of fiery red hair with a beard to match; at least, that's what Babe remembered.

Watching the two women interact tickled Babe. Trinity was outgoing, fun, and energetic, but he knew little about Trinity, the child and teen. Once again, he was at a loss. What kind of girl had she been? He knew all the broad strokes: teenage pregnancy, miscarriage, uneducated, and, as he'd heard others say, wild child. He watched her body language as she heard Lark's story, which was opposite hers. The cute little blonde was Prom Queen material, cheerleader, and most popular with the right crowd. Anything in the social scene, the girl had done it. She had one considerably older brother and wanted to know everything about being the baby in such a big family.

Babe put his arm around her. He looked deep into her eyes, trying to read her emotion. "Trinity Marie, you never mention friends from school. I know I don't, but I'm a peculiar individual, and I know it. You're normal—a loving family, beautiful, and funny."

He tilted his head in curiosity and was engrossed in anything she said. "That's it, big fella, just go right on and rip that band-aid off." She grinned, but he could tell it rang her bell. "Everybody loved Trinity, ma boy. I was one of the most popular girls in my grade until, drum-roll and here it comes, I got pregnant. Parents didn't want their daughters associating with me, as though the condition was contagious. I had to leave school; they couldn't have a preggo near all the sweet little pearls of Jesus. Most of those girls were banging anything with a dick, but they were savvy about it and didn't get caught. No, boy, I was a pariah." She raised her eyebrows. "Once I lost the pregnancy, a couple of girls from school came over. Most everyone rejoiced the mis—" She got choked up and misty-eyed. His heart clenched, and a lump came up his throat. She rubbed her eyes. "Babe, while I knew it was God's way of saying not now, my angel returned to heaven until the time was right. I lost complete trust or desire to have friends; God gave me built-in friends with my sister and brothers. Bethany cried with me and witnessed the emotional, excruciating pain of loss. I told you I didn't have sex again for years. Maybe Joey, yeah, I think it was Joey after we got married. We were in puppy love with no regard for the future, and you know the rest of that story." She took his hand and kissed it. "Don't feel guilty, ma man. It stings, but our little angel, Chancée, is the most precious gift from God, oh and you." She kissed his hand hard and squeezed it.

Mays and Lark were whispering and giggling with each other. Both Babe and Trinity relished Mays' happiness. He was such a good guy and deserved to have his dreams come true. She woke to Babe telling her it was time to wake up. Falling asleep amidst such heartfelt thoughts gave her a restful four-hour nap.

Finally, through customs, baggage claim, and renting a car, the four were on their way to meet Bjorn and Ilsa. Narvik Norway was different than any place Trinity had been. From pointy mountain peaks that soared in the sky to gentler rolls dotted with houses, it seemed like a place for outdoor activities. The greens were greener, and the place felt almost unspoiled. Trinity rambled about seeing the Northern Lights that night and was full of questions.

Babe turned right onto a steep road. Trinity's voice trembled, and she balled her hands in white-knuckled fists. "Boy, you think this vehicle can make it up there." Her voice trembled, "I don't think I like this." He smiled, patted her hand, and kept on going; Trinity was terrified. It was the steepest street she'd ever been on. Mays and Lark were oblivious to anything but themselves. When they neared the highest point, Babe pulled into a rough driveway of sorts aside of one of the larger homes with a pointy peaked roof. That seemed to be the style in the area. Bjorn painted his home a deep rustic red with functional black shutters.

No sooner had they pulled in than a man that could have been taken for Rune, only fifteen years his junior and with a mass of shocking red hair to match his full beard, stepped from the house with arms spread wide. He was a massive man like the brothers. Babe figured the lady beside him was Ilsa. When Bjorn said she was much younger than him, he wasn't kidding.

Ilsa had cascading mahogany waves punctuating her voluptuous figure. While she had a rack the size of the Grand Tetons, her waist couldn't have been more than twenty-four inches. She was stunning with light eyes. Babe had not realized the difference in age between Rune and Bjorn. He figured they were contemporaries, and that's the impression Bjorn was happy to convey. If Babe had to guess, he'd peg him around sixty, and Ilsa would be in her late thirties or early forties.

"Ilsa, would you look at my Viking family?" Babe put out his hand, which Bjorn grasped and drew him into a hug. "Don't tell me, you are Rune's Sonneson, Babe? This fine specimen must be the first-born, grabbing Mays' bicep and forcing a hug. Boys, your grandmother, bless her soul, was a rare beauty; every young man would've taken her as a wife, but my brother was a charmer, and the girl fell in love at first sight. Come on in, and let's get you settled."

Ilsa told him to give the boys a chance to catch their breath. "Unge Kar, uh" she stumbled on her words. "Young men, we insist you stay with family. No need to rent room, Bjorn says; you can Knule to your heart's content right here." She blushed. Bjorn repeated what she had said with a coarse laugh.

"Ha!" Bjorn shouted out. "Get busy," and raised his unkempt eyebrows with a wink and swiveling of his hips.

Babe introduced Trinity and Lark to Bjorn. Mays had collected suitcases from the car, dumping two at Babe's feet. Ilsa brought them to the guest room and another room resembling a hobby or sewing room with two twin beds. Babe gave Mays the guest room with a full-size bed and took the twin beds for him and Trinity.

The stairs were narrow and steep. Babe walked in front of Trinity, telling her to hop on his back if it was too hard on her legs. *Fat chance of that*, he thought to himself. The six began hospitality hour with a bottle of Audny, Norway's most popular single malt. The pouring commenced, including a side of crusty bread and what looked like brown cheese. Their uncle emptied his glass in one deep gulp, ending with a rip-roaring exclamation, then poured another. Mays and Lark kept up with the older guy while Trinity and Babe slowly sipped theirs. It wasn't long before Bjorn, Mays, and Lark were blotto.

Ilsa ordered everyone to the dining table. Trinity asked, "Do you mind me asking what this dish is?" Babe told her always to expect root vegetables and cured lamb or fish. The dinner she prepared was smoked salmon atop what appeared to be mashed or pureed potato. The name of the dish rolled off the woman's tongue, but Trinity didn't want to butcher it too much but smiled instead of words. "Babe, it's not etouffee," she laughed. Trinity raised her glass of beer, "Here's to tasting new food." Following dinner, Ilsa put a cone-like dessert in the middle of the table. It looked like rings of pastry stacked and was scrumptious. The guys returned to the living area while Trinity and Lark helped Ilsa with the dishes.

Lark needed to sit. Trinity watched as the girl swayed. "Lark, go sit with Mays." Obviously, doing dishes and cleaning up after dinner was not in the girl's wheelhouse. Besides, she was having a hard time with too much alcohol. Trinity pictured Mays, in his condition, navigating the steep staircase.

Ilsa's command of English was better than expected. Now and then, she'd get flustered by a word; however, she managed to get the idea across.

Seeing Lark having difficulty maneuvering from the kitchen to the living room, Babe got up to give her hand to Mays, who was also half-baked. He had visions of his brother climbing the steps; it was hard enough sober.

Lark immediately started talking, "What have y'all been talking about?" She closed her eyes and turned toward Babe, acting almost childlike. "What was it like being a Marine? Like what kind of things did you have to do? I'm so interested; I've never met—"

Before she said soldier, Babe stayed calm but answered, "Lark, it's not what one would call an appropriate topic of conversation. It was Hell, and we'll leave it there." He could only think, thank God his wife wasn't in the room; she may have been harsh. It annoyed the shit out of her when her brothers would ask questions about things he'd seen and done, and she responded to them with a 'shut the fuck up' or 'none of your business.'

"Oh, sorry. I hope I didn't offend you." The corners of her mouth weren't the usual glistening dimpled smile. Lark was embarrassed and looked like she would break down in tears. "Forgive me, Babe?" He tipped his head slightly, acknowledging her apology. Maybe when she was sober, he'd tell her like he did the boys: just say thank you for your service or say nothing at all. He had told Mays enough when they were in the steam room; he could convey stories about his brother and explain the dos and don'ts.

It turned out that Ilsa had an itinerary for her visitors, including hikes, visiting the fjords, and three-day excursions to Finland and Sweden. She had already made all the reservations, filling every day and evening. While eating at a local favorite one night, they sat at a window. The sky glowed as though from the heavens. "Babe, look!" Trinity bubbled. "It's beautiful and wondrous. Ilsa, I'm sure it is old hat to you, but thanks for placing us in the perfect place to watch the brilliance of the Northern Lights."

She threw her head back with an explosive laugh, " Never tire; those are our gods showing their mighty power. We must give thanks to them constantly." That was a new one for Trinity, the devout Catholic girl. It didn't seem like she was kidding, and not wanting to insult, Trinity wanted to ask if she was being silly or if it was lore. Thinking back about some of the artwork and wooden figures in their home, it dawned on her that they represented Odin, Thor, and Loki, which she had seen on the TV series Vikings. *Ask Babe later*, she thought.

Ilsa and Bjorn carried on like newlyweds—kissing constantly and nuzzling into each other. There was no doubt that Bjorn liked his alcohol, beer, or wine and managed to tie one on every night. He wasn't a sloppy drunk and seemed to have his wits about him, but they had watched him polish off a tremendous amount of Vodka. He spread both his arms up and out. "So, my brother's Sonneson, what do you think of the homeland?

Can you feel the courage and strength of our ancestors? You two," pointing to Babe and Mays, "Would have been a force. You'll see what I mean tomorrow when we go to a museum. It'll scratch that yearning itch you've had all your lives."

Later that night, Trinity asked Babe as they lay in the pushed-together twin beds, constantly fighting the gap. "Do you think they are Pagan and believe all that stuff like different gods and Valhalla?" She curled against him.

"I don't know. Valhalla is what we call Heaven, I guess. Don't try to convert them to Catholicism. You've already scored quite a few for God— me, for one; I was hopeless, and the boys, they'd seen Hell up close and personal. Look at them now. So, don't venture into religion—Period. Now," and he pulled her onto him, shedding her top over her head. "Like you say, let's get busy."

Max met Gwen at Mandina's. Her spunky red hair suited her well. The detective was totally smitten and hung onto her every word. They laughed and talked like they were the only people in the restaurant. At first, it was a casual, carefree conversation about the weather, the traffic, and even a dabble into politics. "So, Detective Max, what is your story? How'd you get into police work?" She gazed into his eyes, which sent shivers down his spine. *Good tingles or not so good,* he pondered. They weren't like anything he ever felt before. Was it love or warning?

He answered it was boring and nothing to write home about, emphasizing that it wasn't like TV drama. It was similar to a family business that started with his great-grandfather. She grilled him about the worst cases and asked if he had a method for finding criminals. Work was the one thing he didn't want to talk about. He lived it; why talk about it? He shifted the subject a few times, but she always drew him back to law enforcement. It got under his skin.

"Gwen, what brought you to New Orleans?" She couldn't remember if she'd made up some lie or what she had said previously. Whether she said it before or not, falling back on a relationship gone bad was always a good answer. "I get that. You been married? I have two ex-wives. Being married to the blue line is hard, and unless you've always lived the life, it's known to create many failed marriages. The longer one is in the force, the more involved in the job and family life fades into the background." She wanted to know about his ex-wives. Was it cheating, fighting, loneliness, or money? Max had to think about the answer because the fact was it wasn't any of the above. Bored was the best description. It boiled down to the fact that they lived separate lives and only communicated between the sheets. He hoped he didn't offend.

She giggled and said, "Heck, no. So many people think that great sex is love. Sex is just a physical response to hitting the right pleasure points. Some people know it instinctively, while others need a map. So, Max Sledge, do you need a map?" He could feel the tips of his ears burning, which meant they were probably bright red. The bulge in his pants didn't help matters. If she was the kind of girl looking to get laid on a first date, she wasn't the girl for him. He'd been there and done that. Boner or not, it wasn't happening.

Max could see disappointment register on her face, but her forwardness was over the top. He wanted to build a relationship and then come what may. He had enough clean call girls to satisfy any needs, they gave him the cop discount, and there was none of the call-me-in-the-morning.

IF AT FIRST YOU DON'T SUCCEED

*7*rey and Max worked tirelessly on the new murders haunting New Orleans. There was little to no evidence other than hashed-up bodies. The killer du jour was, if anything, thorough. Trey massaged his temples, "It's obvious it was part of some insane sexual deviance. Each bed shows signs of sex but not one hair, smear of lubricant, or body fluid. Nobody can be that thorough. We're missing something, Max. Let's go back through the reports."

They compared the approximate time of death; there wasn't a pattern there. They checked and double-checked all the information they had, and up to that point, the only consistency was a weapon. The sicko used a nine-inch blade, probably from a set of kitchen knives. It wasn't like indicators were pointing to hunting or combat knives, once more leaning the assumption to a female serial killer. Susie Homemaker to Aileen Wournos sounded like the kind of vast change in the woman's personality. Obviously, she was demented by maybe something freaky, like multiple personalities.

"I want you to meet Gwen. I get weird vibes; I don't know if it's love or sensory warnings." He rocked back in his chair, hands clasped behind his head. "I'd like to think she's just that into me that I ain't had that kinda attention in a long time, so it feels strange. She wanted to jump in the sack on the first date. What's up with that?" He scuffed his feet as he rocked back and forth. Trey had never seen him so captured by a woman.

Trey read over the information provided by the Memphis investigators. "It's the way of the world, almost like a handshake," Max grunted with displeasure in response. "I want a face-to-face with the investigator on the case. Hopefully, Big Jim will approve or, at the very least, bring him down here." The notes were thorough and matched to a tee the crime scenes they had processed. The killer was methodical and careful, not leaving anything behind. To his surprise, the captain approved the field trip to Tennessee.

Trey called the contact in Memphis, a man named Duke Wallace. He had a strong twang, and all Trey could visualize was some country western singer. The man answered, "Wallace. How can I help you?" He was polite to the point Trey felt it was duplicitous.

"Hello. It's Trey Kimble from the New Orleans Police Department. I am flying into Memphis the day after tomorrow. I know you sent me everything you had on your Aileen Wuornos impersonator, but maybe if I follow the trail of victims and talk to people in those areas, I might glean something that will help me stop the murders here." The man couldn't have been more accommodating and offered to walk him literally through the mess. Saying a different perspective may just be what they needed. So, the politeness was just his way.

With Trey in Memphis, Max found himself either up to his neck in paperwork or with a wandering mind. Gwen was too pretty for him, yet she dug the shit out of him. She'd call at least three or four times a day since their date night and had lunch a couple of times, but the nighttime dates were still at one. He muffled his voice when he called; he didn't want to be the subject of gossip. "Hey, pretty lady. How's your day going? I started thinking, we haven't been to dinner again, so how about tonight, if you're not too busy? We could maybe meet for an early supper at Liuzza's. You game?" They talked for another fifteen minutes and made plans to meet at six.

Max watched the clock, and time went exceptionally slow. There hadn't been another murder in a week, which seemed strange, especially how the others came fast. Hopefully, the sicko moved on. Truth be told, he hoped the murderer was still in town, and he could catch them or at least put an end to the mania, perhaps sparing many other lives from a heinous, vicious death. The perpetrator obviously had some anger issues, or, and his stomach revolted in a gut twist, she got off on the knife penetrating the victim's body.

He decided if Gwen became too forward, he would be honest and tell her his stance on rushing into sex. She may dismiss him, which would end it, or she'd appreciate his sincerity.

Promptly at five-thirty, he left for the day. He wondered what they'd talk about. So far, at the one dinner, she was hyped into wanting to hear about his world. The lunches were more her complaining about her boss and eating. It wasn't like they could pass the afternoon away gabbing; they were both on the clock.

Liuzza's was a staple; most of the locals frequented it, and usually, there were only a couple of unfamiliar faces—everyone knew everyone or someone who knew them. Max arrived early. He overheard the chatter, and it was all about the serial murderer. He'd see a finger pointed in his direction and knew they all wanted to ask him about the newest drama. Charlie, an oldtimer, sat at Max' table. The gang at Mandina's knew better than to ask about police news. Occasionally, one had a pestering neighbor or a ticket; maybe this was a personal matter. Charlie sat still with an intense look. "I know you can't say anything, but you can nod. Y'all closing in on the killer?"

Max closed his eyes, meaning no. "Now, Charlie, you know I ain't gonna talk to you about police business. I advise you to stay faithful to your wife and don't go straying with a flirtatious young thing. You'll stay healthy that way. Mert would crack you with a fryin' pan." The two had a chuckle. He watched as his redhead love interest parked her car and entered the restaurant. Something about her wasn't as appealing as before; maybe it was the sickening feeling of thinking about the hideous murders. Gwen had a determined look on her face and not the usual effervescent, bubbly lightness.

Max stood as she approached. He made polite introductions, and Charlie took the hint and returned to his seat, where those around him jawed and pushed for answers. She faked an upturn of the lips, hardly authentic. "What you two gabbing about? Let me guess, it's not the weather or the stock market; how about the latest intriguing news?"

The detective shook his head, saying everyone knew not to talk about police business with him unless they had a particular personal problem. Work was his least favorite subject; he lived it. Gwen inwardly laughed about how ironic it would be to turn Max from a friendly date to her next conquest. She could tell he fancied himself and his partner as top-notch detectives, and here she was right under his nose. "How was your day?" he asked, trying to cut the awkwardness of silence. "What's your boss like? Young, old, nice, ornery? Look over the menu while you think. Everything here is good eatin'. Let's start with onion rings, and I'm gonna have their seafood pladda—it's uge." Like so many locals, he didn't pronounce the h in huge. Gwen went for the Eggplant Napoleon and then started asking about his day. "No, ma'am, I been lookin' forward to your company, and I'm not gonna muck it up with work. I'm down for a frosty glass draft and listening about your day." She was getting frustrated. "Gwen, no offense, but the piece of shit psycho isn't gonna ruin our dinna."

Her eyes changed from piqued curiosity to seething. "How do you know if she's been the victim one time too many and is striking out?" The venom dripped from her words. Saved by the onion rings. *Curious*, he thought. She referred to the killer as a woman; the news still referred to the killer as a man or kept it gender-neutral. Perhaps she had been a victim of abuse and needed help. *I ain't no shrink and need to leave it alone.* Max changed the subject and told her the history of the restaurant. Her mind was elsewhere, probably still engrossed in the serial murders. "Max, tell me about the murders. How did you feel seeing the bodies? How do you deal with the gore?"

He drew his hand down his face, stretching the jowls. *Fuck it.* "I told ya I don't like talkin' work." He glanced out the window. "It's called compartmentalizing. You separate yourself from feeling. It's a puzzle, and as long as I keep my emotions out of the scene, I go through the situation and facts like a dog gnawing his favorite bone. For someone like you, for instance, it's beyond gruesome. I don't care how fucked over someone feels; nobody has the right to take another life. These are premeditated and sick. End of story." Gwen's expression hadn't changed throughout his answer. As sweet as she seemed, there was something dark in her—maybe a lousy breakup or abuse as a child. Whatever the situation was, it colored her bleak.

The seafood platter came in time; he turned his attention to the heaping plate of food. "There's so much here; feel free to help yourself. It's delicious."

The rest of their dinner was without incident. From then on, all the conversations were food-related and about upcoming festivals. The night was drawing to a close. "Will you walk me to the car?" She tipped her head toward her shoulder. The car was a few steps away; why play the femme fatale? He wasn't going to tell her no.

At her car, she wrapped her arms around him and looked with willingness into his eyes. He kissed her gently on the lips and pulled away after. "I hope you enjoyed your dinner."

"I wish I could say we could go to my place for dessert, but I live with—"

Max shifted back and forth. "My answer would have been the same. It's premature for anything other than a sweet good night kiss."

With a pout, she retorted, "Do you not find me attractive? Or do you have issues in the sack?" She was pressing all the pressure points, especially questioning about getting an erection.

He avoided her gaze, "Of course, I think you are attractive. You're a pretty girl, Gwen, with an outrageous body." He looked her in the eyes, "As far as pecker problems, thank God, so far so good. We'll get down to business in due time." He gave her a quick peck on the lips and told her to drive carefully; he'd talk to her the following day. He watched as she started her car and pulled away. He slid into the unit and said out loud. "Where's Trey when you need him?"

Duke Wallace, the investigator from the Memphis Homicide division, and Trey were about the same age, somewhere in the thirties. He was of similar height and build. His hair appeared dark, at least the part poking out from his cowboy hat. He had an angular face. With a name like Duke, Trey expected the man to be bigger, like John Wayne. The two hit it off right from the start.

Duke established a timeline with as many particulars as he had accumulated in the investigation. After a long day, Duke took Trey to his favorite watering hole. "You ever ride a mechanical bull?" Trey's phone dinged with a text from Max. It was a picture of his flame and him at Liuzza's. Trey held it up to show Duke. "What the hay? That girl gets around. She lived around these parts not too long ago. It was a cluster from the beginning. The girl, Gwen Peters, as I recall, was hot and heavy with the Shelby boy. His family practically owns most of the bars and other businesses in Memphis. The boy was great if he wasn't drinking, but what an idiot with a few cocktails. He drank until he was slobbering drunk and would pick fights, you know what I mean. I'm sure you have more than your fair share."

He went on to talk about the poor girl having problems with the boy. He beat her one night when he was drunk, and she accidentally killed him; then, a while later, her aunt and uncle, who she lived with, died. No one knew where she went; she disappeared. He guessed she was tired of people gawking at her and whispering behind her back.

"Did she tell you the boy beat her up?"

"No doubt. Gwen had bruises on her face and a slice along her jawline." Duke slugged down his beer. He called the bartender, "Chuck, this girl look familiar to you?" He held up Trey's phone.

"Damn, Son, that's the girl hooked up with Dwayne. She was a cute little thing. What happened to her? I done heard she killed him, but you remember how hot-tempered he was when he'd thrown back a few. But she was a little strange. She came across as sweet but had a crazy look in her eyes. She didn't trust no one. Want another?" He pointed to the empty mug. After watching the people riding the mechanical bull, they headed out. Once in the car, Trey texted Max.

Trey: Padna, your girl has a history. Be careful.

Max: Like how? NM call me in an hour.

Trey: Don't jump in the sack with her. I got a feeling.

Max: 10-4

It wasn't like Trey to talk about Max' sex life; however, Max was always eager to chide Trey. The older detective wasn't as polished, not that Trey was wreaking posh. Something about her past, the sketchy slayings, and a trend developing in NOLA created an itch he couldn't quite scratch.

Trey opened the conversation. "So, she wiped every crime scene down. I don't know that our crime lab would dust the nobs on the sink or prints on the toilet lever. It's always the little things. There's no such thing as a perfect murder; I have to keep reminding myself. I don't believe in coincidences, and strangely, she landed in New Orleans when y'all's murders stopped and ours began. If anything, it's food for thought. My partner is head over heels with this girl, and he doesn't date per se. Max is a kick-ass detective, but you know how it is when the heart enters the picture—you get blinded by love." He used air quotes on the word love.

They returned to the police station to check the evidence. Trey saw a long blonde hair in one of the bags. Duke responded, "from a wig." His eyebrows arched reflexively. Trey didn't say it but felt that the NOLA crime techs were more conscientious. Duke had been right; there wasn't much to see. So far, the most significant assist was Chuck's I.D. of Gwen and then the story about the self-defense accident resulting in the death of Dwayne Shelby. The chick definitely was missing some cards from the deck. Of all the ladies in New Orleans, it was just Max' luck to pick a serial killer. He knew he'd need to change the line of thinking; there was nothing linking the girl to any of the slayings. Everything was coincidental, but it was hard to let go when things seemed to fall into place.

The following morning, he wanted to talk to known friends of the victims. He struck out; nobody could identify Gwen. The only friends left to question were Leo's. Duke said they'd talked to the wife, but she didn't know anything and was an emotional wreck. "Duke, you mind if we question her again?"

Duke drove down a street that could have been in New Orleans with shotgun houses set like dominos block after block. He pulled up to a blue house. "Let's hope she's not drunk," the Memphis investigator warned.

Before they reached the door, a young woman dressed in a housecoat and slippers greeted them. "I done told you once, I don't know none of his friends. Leo was a kind-hearted man, but all he left me was two mouths to feed. At least the house is paid off, but I still gotta keep the lights on."

Trey stepped forward, "My name is Trey Kimble from New Orleans, Louisiana. Anything you can tell me about Leo's habits?"

She was quick to answer, "Mista, Leo didn't have no habits. He liked to go to the barbeque bar and get us some ribs and chicken sometimes. He liked to dance." She smiled, "And boy, could that man dance." She closed her eyes with a smile as though remembering better times when they'd go dancing. "That's what caught my eye. I was young, and the owner let me waitress for tips, but I'd watch him. He might have friends at the bar that I don't know about, ya know?"

They thanked her for her time and made their way to the bar. "She's right, they have lip-smacking ribs."

Trey could smell the tempting aroma of meat on the pit. The bar wasn't open, but they saw a back screened-in porch, figuring someone was back there tending to the pit. A burly, light-skinned man in a smudged white apron spoke, "We not open yet, boys."

Duke spoke up, "Can we have a moment of your time; we'll be quick." The man nodded and walked toward them. Trey held out the picture of Max and Gwen.

A broad smile formed on the man's face. "I don't know the fella and the lady I seen once. Damn why she cut her long blonde hair so short. She still looks good, but Becky, from Nashville, turned every man's head when she came to the bar. Quite a few offered to buy her a drink and asked her to dance, but she shut them all down and danced by herself. One of our frequent fliers, Leo, a slick dancing dude with Michael Jackson moves, asked her to dance, and she did. They was rolling bodies, if you get my meaning. I ain't seen her in a spell. Where she at?"

Duke and Trey hopped in the car and took off. Trey spoke first, "Damn, whatever was cooking smelled fantastic. I guess we came away with an answer to one question about the blonde strand from the wig. Gwen, evidently, takes on different names, looks, and backstories. There's no pinpointing what we're looking for, making an APB useless. At least I know how to reach her." They surmised she had killed Leo. She had no M.O. Anybody could be her next victim.

Duke dropped him at the airport. Trey had an hour to wait until boarding and called Max, who answered immediately. "Isn't this a fucked up situation? The one girl that strikes my interest is fuckin' psycho." Trey explained about the wig and the story of the boyfriend igniting the monster within her. It had become a game to see how far she could go. They agreed that she hadn't even considered the consequences. "We gotta devise a plan. I know how to catch her, but I'm not thrilled at the prospect. I don't wanna be fuckin' somebody with boys in the closet; I'll never hear the end of my white flabby ass. She keeps asking me to have sex, really pushing the point.

I could agree and take her to my house, ain't nobody there. You and a couple others could hide in my closet. It's got louvas, so ya can kinda see and spring out before she stabs me. At least I know it's coming. None of the others had a clue. I'd know ahead; therefore, the upper hand. I'm not letting her tie me up or anything too kinky. What if she doesn't attack; y'all would just have a peep show. Lemme think this through."

While at first, he'd felt a strong attraction to her like the best thing since sliced bread, Gwen's peculiar personality, almost to the point of obsession, dulled his interest, but he was starting to get a clearer picture. The ultimate euphoria would be to get an officer of the law. What a slap in the face to the blue line.

Trey laughed aloud, "You drunk? You know it couldn't go down at your place, nor would anyone be hiding in your closet. We'd have I.T. set you up at a pre-planned location. I got it," he exclaimed, "Hotel Noelle will cooperate with us, no problem. We got the Babe-Trinity hook-up. Since the hotel is so old, a locked door connects some of their rooms. The team would be next door, and you'd hardly be naked and sure as shit wouldn't be doing the wild thing. Oldtimer, it'll go down with precision. The surveillance system they're using now is insane. We'll be able to see and hear everything y'all say and do, and you'll be able to communicate with us. Sorry no getting a piece of ass on company time." He laughed again. "We can work out all the details when I get to work tomorrow."

"Hey, Trey-hole, who the fuck you callin' Oldtimer?"

NEXT STOP, HOME

*T*he holiday was ending. Babe and Trinity were chomping at the bit to get home to Chancée and the boys. Trinity kept pace with everyone. Between the complexities of life- stories shared over Vodka, pints of beer, or anything alcoholic, they all had a chance to tell something to capture the group's attention. No doubt, jaws dropped when Trinity shared the ordeal of psycho woman and the recovery, although Babe had to fill in much of the coma time with her progression as she wasn't in a present state of mind at the time.

Trinity had pictures of everything from the shaggy, dirty street kids to Louie's, with Babe sitting in his spot and then all the people who worked there. She had many candid shots from the wedding photos of her siblings. Trinity paused over the picture of Chance; she choked up and couldn't tell the story. Babe gave a sprinted explanation. He remembered Chance and Trinity looking alike, but seeing the picture served to solidify that opinion.

It wasn't long before the captain announced their descent. Lark and Mays had a two-hour layover to catch their flight back to Atlanta. The holiday was fun, but getting home wasn't fast enough. With hugs and well wishes, the two couples went their way; Mays and Lark went to the bar, and Babe and Trinity headed home.

Once in the car, zipping onto the interstate, the radio personality went into a full news alert and said the police found another body and then proceeded with a brief overview of the current terror in the city. "Oh my God, Babe, another serial killer. That's gonna hit Louie's and the hotel hard; summer is slow to start with. What's wrong with people?"

Babe called Trey. "What the fuck is going on? We've been out of town—"

"Oh, I'm well aware, big guy. This new killing spree is twisted, like Aileen Wuornos. Babe, it's sick—There is no pattern; she just kills on a whim. I think it's some kind of sexual thing. All the men have been left naked in a blood-stained bed with their chests chopped up bad, like ground beef."

Babe's mind went wandering. The last serial killer, Carlton, had been somewhat easy because he kept his hunt in the French Quarter, honing in mostly on prostitutes. The tone in Trey's voice suggested there was more to the story. *Not mine to do,* he reminded himself. Why wasn't it; so, they picked up the wrong woman and got themselves killed. It wasn't like they fell prey and were helpless. The men sought what they expected as pleasure. Just for shits and giggles, he'd look over the file if asked, but he wasn't putting himself purposefully in the mix. Trinity would appreciate the decision.

"Babe, you still there?" The silence had been awkward.

The big guy cleared his throat, "Yes, we landed about an hour ago and are now on our way home. Why?"

"I wanna pick your brain. I'm not asking you to get involved; Big Jim would fire my ass." Trey chuffed. "For sure, especially being you. Long story there."

Decision time. Babe didn't want his home to be on anyone's radar, but it couldn't hurt if Trey knew. He had no desire to go up to Louie's; all he wanted was to stay home; it'd been too long away from the boys and princess. With all intuition saying no and abundant red flags waving like mad, he gave Trey his address, boldly saying it wasn't common knowledge and to keep the info under his hat.

Trinity looked at him with disbelief. "So you won't give my family our address, but Trey? Whateva. I was thinkin'—"

Babe put his hands to his head with a sarcastic grin, "Uh-oh. Thinking again, are you? Girl, we're in trouble now." She slapped his arm as they turned onto Chestnut. In seconds, they were home, and the boys came running from the house. Trinity had taken many photos and picked up souvenirs for everyone at the house, including Ruthie and her sister.

Once inside, questions began at a racetrack pace. Trinity relieved Ruthie of Chancée. "She's grown so much. I knew the teeth were coming, but the two bottoms broke through, and I missed them. I hope she hasn't been too fussy." Trinity pouted with exaggeration. She ran her finger along the top, and her eyes widened, "but I'll be here for the top two; they're about to break through." The boys asked non-stop questions; Trinity handed Reg her phone, "I know you know the code," as she smothered the baby with kisses and cuddles.

"Who doesn't? It doesn't take a brainiac to figure out 2223, otherwise known as B-A-B-E. I'm surprised you don't have it tattooed on your a—" Trinity shot a look that shouted, control your mouth. Reg threw his arm in the air with a sigh of exasperation. "I was going to say arm. What did you think I was gonna say?" She raised an eyebrow; she knew full well he was going to slip and say ass. The doorbell rang, and she heard Babe say he had it.

Reg and Jake continued swiping through the pictures, commenting on the high mountain peaks. They started laughing, almost unable to breathe. She pulled the phone to see what they were carrying on about. It was a picture of Bjorn. Jake queried, "Is that dude for real, or is he a photo op?" Trinity smiled and nodded that he was real. "He looks like a character from the Vikings show, Lord of the Rings, or a troll with crazy-colored wild stand-up hair." Trinity giggled to herself. Bjorn was most definitely a character, as was his Ilsa, and yes, she was a Pagan and worshipped the wooden figures. The customs in that part of the world were fascinating, like something from a movie, and utterly foreign to her.

Ruthie and Sarah were thrilled with the Norwegian sweaters and even more so with the postcards. "Trinity, where's your husband?" Ruthie spoke softly. She told the woman they were safe to talk without prying ears. " If you say so, we had a visitor one evening." She put her hand to her mouth, whispering. "It was CJ, Chris' father. I could tell who he was; the boy resembled him. He was polite and apologized for coming without notice. He was a nice-looking man, a bit weathered but pleasant enough. I know Chris is gonna tell your husband, but I'd like to be the one to talk to him first since I was in charge of the comings and goings of the household while y'all were traveling." Trinity nodded; she'd want to do the same thing. It was the adult thing to do. While the experience was phenomenal, it was also good to be home.

Trey was wide-eyed with a dropped jaw as he glanced around the foyer, formal living, and dining rooms. "These are your digs? Wow, it's something. I had no idea—"

With his half-cocked smile, Babe interrupted, "This was my grandfather's home, and when he died, he left everything to me. I miss the old guy; he was one of a kind. I'd gladly go back to my tiny barren apartment if I could have him back again." He tipped his head to the left. "Follow me to the study before the boys are all up in your business. They're nosy bastards."

The detective followed Babe while keeping his head on a swivel, checking the place out. "W-wait, boys? Y'all had a girl, right?"

Babe said yes and went into how the boys fit in the picture. He thought he'd already told Trey about the boys, but maybe it was Max, *whatever*, he thought. Once in the study, Babe went to close the doors when Ruthie poked her head in. "Just checking to see if you and your company would like anything from the kitchen or bar." *Fat chance, Ruthie, you wanted to see who came over*, he smiled inwardly at her protective ways.

Trey ran his hand through his hair. The night kept getting stranger.

"Sorry to interrupt, suga; I'm here to help with the family." She looked the man up and down, trying to get a read. "I was Mr. Rune's caretaker; I guess I just came with the house. The name is Ruthie and you are?" She raised her eyebrows with a sweet smile.

Trey was stumbling on his thoughts, not sure what to say, when Babe chimed in, "Ruthie, this is Detective Trey Kimble of the NOPD. He was a big help during the, uh, Trinity's ordeal. You want something?" he asked Trey. "Drink, beer, food?" He smiled at the old gal, "Ruthie, can you grab two beers and a box of crackers? Please tell my wife we'll be out there in a bit." She arranged a cheese and crackers tray rather than tossing a box.

The door was promptly closed as soon as Ruthie brought the beer and tray. Trey told Babe the story of Gwen, the Memphis murders, the different personas, and the New Orleans murders, finishing up with the finale that she was dating Max.

Babe dragged his hand down his face, stretching the skin slightly as though contemplative. The sentiment was the same between the two men: poor Max finds a lady he likes, and she ends up being a suspected serial killer. He listened to Trey, tapping his fingers on an arm of his chair. Babe's mind created a picture montage, trying to fit all the pieces in. It most assuredly was a cluster. "Needless to say, big guy, it's a fucking mess and creating an uncomfortable vibe. It's not like she has a type of victim." He used air quotes. He tipped the bottle for a swig. "We have a plan, but it's dodgy. We gotta be careful of entrapment; you know all the pain-in-the-ass rules for law enforcement, it's like the rules protect the criminals."

They agreed to meet the following day with Max. Leaving the study, the clamoring of feet on stair treads elicited a clearing of Babe's throat. Reg and Jake came to an abrupt halt, noticing the stranger. Eyes fixed on the new guy and mouths agape, Babe addressed them, "Better close your mouth, or our guest will think y'all are a coupla simpletons. We'll be in the family room if you want to join us."

Trey mentioned he remembered the youngest boy, now fourteen, from the pack of street kids. Babe nodded. The couch and chairs were overstuffed and felt fluffy like a cloud. The kind one sits in and has trouble getting up; it sucks the person in. "I'm still reeling over your place, Babe. Steph and I have a small place in Tremé. I get you don't want people to know where you live, and I won't tell anyone except Steph." He flared his fingers out expressively.

Babe explained it wasn't like that; there were extenuating circumstances. Trinity popped in from the kitchen, "Yeah, like he doesn't want my family to know where we live." Her voice raised an octave. " Who says that?" She raised an eyebrow and put a hand on her hip with a questioning but scolding look. "It's not like they'd park their ass on the couch, but it's asinine. He knows where they live." She handed Chanceé to Babe. "He can't deny this one, that's for sure." The pigment in her skin had gotten darker, hardly noticeable unless she was next to Reg, whose complexion was lily-white, and then the contrast was glaring. She was a light caramel with dark hair and striking blue eyes. Her tiny turned-up nose and her full rosy puckers were like Trinity's. "She's getting to be a big girl with two bottom teeth and the top two about to break through." Trinity plopped on the sofa. "Did Babe tell you about Norway? That's where we went, to meet his Great-Uncle Bjorn." She had her phone out in a flash and swiped through pictures showing Trey.

"That's some red hair. The blond guy has to be related to you, Babe. Jesus, Mary, and Joseph, you two dudes are—"

"I call them bookends," Trinity interrupted. Trey tilted his head, sticking his bottom lip out while nodding contemplatively. He agreed with the description.

Trey visited for about an hour, spoke with the two boys, and even held the baby for a few minutes. He would have never considered Babe "uptown" in his wildest dream. It didn't fit. There were pictures and paintings of his grandfather and grandmother. Trey couldn't help but speak about a striking familial resemblance. The evening concluded with setting a time for the three, Trey, Babe, and Max, to meet. It had to be stealthy; any word to the captain and the detectives would be in deep shit. The speculation: James

"Big Jim" Campbell, the new captain, slid down a few rungs, not being the biggest, baddest motherfucker in the room; he was intimidated by Babe.

In the chambers of his mind, the big guy recalled meeting the captain, who prided himself on the improvements he brought to the Memphis police. Babe weighed a thought. *Was the captain in Memphis during the rash of murders, or had he already moved? Maybe that's why he'd been agreeable to Trey going to Memphis.* He wanted one of his detectives to solve the case, and since they hadn't resolved it in Memphis, he'd put his NOLA team on it.

On parting, Babe mentioned that the captain coming from Memphis was food for thought. Maybe he knew Gwen or her family. "Trey, is it all circumstantial or coincidental? For one, I don't believe in coincidence. There is more to this captain than meets the eye." Trey shrugged, but Babe could tell it also sparked the cogs in his brain—*research time.*

He heard Ruthie in the kitchen; she called out, and he followed the voice. "Sir, that policeman friend of yours is a nice-looking young man. Speaking of nice-looking," she inhaled deeply, trying to segue, "We had a visitor while y'all were traveling." She seemed nervous, with a slight tremble in her voice. "I hope you're not angry with me."

Babe smiled as he grabbed a can of beer from the fridge, "Now, didn't I tell you no family barbecues?" She slapped him on the arm and giggled. He had lightened the atmosphere.

Ruthie's shoulders dropped, and she seemed more at ease. "CJ, Chris' father, came to see the boy. He's a nice man, and Chris is his spitting image."

To Ruthie's surprise, Babe responded, "Good, good. I was hoping. I take it all went well?" She smiled and nodded, saying Chris was bound to tell him—conversation over.

Babe and Trinity closed the house tight for the night and went to their room with the baby. "Now I think your last words before entering the house were, 'I was thinkin'.'"

Trinity sat on the bed. "I think it's about time we have a party here and invite my family, maybe Trey and Max, Shep—" He started to interrupt, but she shushed him. It's not like anyone is trying to steal the kids or come after me. Just think about it, okay?"

He knew she'd bug him until he consented, so he decided to waive the white flag and let her do whatever she wanted. At that moment, his mind was on the shit going on with Max, and he questioned if there was any connection to the captain—probably not. It was odd that the new captain was from Memphis, and the suspected killer was as well. Yes, there probably were coincidences in most people's worlds, but never, so far, in his. The recent serial killer started her spree in Memphis. The timing of their arrival in New Orleans was strange, and there were lit strobes of warning in his mind. Memphis was a big city, and it was like someone asking him if he knew one of their friends who was a Marine, as if with over one hundred seventy thousand. He wasn't saying he thought the man had anything to do with the slayings, but maybe he knew the woman in some way.

After putting the baby in the crib, Babe met Trinity as she quietly closed the door to the nursery. He had an eager look in his eyes and began relieving her of her clothes. "Just trying to help," he smirked. "I've missed our bed."

SUSPICIONS

*D*riving to meet Trey and Max, Babe couldn't help but reflect on everything that had happened since leaving the Corps; the list was long. Surely most people didn't have the kind of shit he had. Was it that trouble followed him, or did he create it? There wasn't constant drama during his time of service, but, in all fairness, they were in the thick of disaster at every turn, and yes, it was life and death. Everybody was in the boiling pot, not just him. If anything, he had brought order during those times.

Parking in the Quarter was always a pain in the ass, but Trey's decision to meet at Café du Monde was a parking nightmare. He knew he could park at Hotel Noelle but didn't want anyone to think he was milking the privilege. *Fuck it.* He pulled into the parking garage at the same time as Louis, one of Trinity's brothers. "Hey, Vic. The family is glad y'all are back. I bet it was a stellar experience. My sister talked to Mama and didn't let her off the phone for half an hour, and Trinity did all the talking. She said we'll see the photos on Sunday." *Ah, yes, Sunday dinner*, he pondered.

Louis headed into the hotel, and Babe hoofed it to Café du Monde, which was only a three-block stroll. He arrived before the detectives. Sitting on the other side was a perky redhead with A.D.D. issues; the girl couldn't sit still. Max showed up, and cute red waved while he didn't acknowledge Babe. *Okay, stealth mode.* Ten minutes later, Trey showed up and sat with Babe, not glancing at Max.

Under his breath, Trey said, "Max wanted you to put eyes on his friend and see if your alarm bells were set into motion. He thinks you have some extra sense when it comes to criminals." Both men stifled a laugh. Trey ordered his coffee and beignets. "Steph would be so pissed if she knew I was here. She's been bugging me to come down to the levee and watch the sun come up with coffee and beignets. We now will have the little one in tow, so it won't be quite as romantic as it would've been, but such is the deal, right?"

With raised brows and a crooked smile, Babe agreed. "You got that right. The little red chick has either a serious case of A.D.D., is ramped up on drugs, or nervous with a purpose. Have you seen her before, or is this your first glance?" He asked the detective. Trey showed Babe the photo Max had sent him again. "Same freakin' boots. Tell your pal to offer a foot massage. The way she keeps touching the right one tells me she's got something in it—Drugs, money, possibly a weapon." They were too far away from the conversation to hear anything, but the young woman was not overjoyed. Max laid his palm on the table, which caused it to clatter. "Whoa, look at her eyes. She wanted something, and he said no. She is livid; all that's missing is smoke coming out of her ears."

Trey laughed and told him about her pushing Max for sex, pressing all the insecurity buttons, like can't get it up, or he's—" He held up his hand and moved his baby finger, insinuating— and he raised his eyebrows and chuckled. "He totally frustrates her, which speaks volumes to me. I ask myself, why is she so persistent; it's not like she couldn't find someone to do the job. No, I think she wants a cop."

"Possible," Babe tilted his head and took the last bite of his morning treat. The woman put some money on the table and left in a huff. Max took the check, left her money on the table, and approached them. Shaking Trey's hand and Babe's as though acquaintances.

With a smile glued on his face, Trey asked what the huffiness was all about. "Same thing. She asked if she could spend the night at my place. I said not yet. What is it with this chick? Had she not been so pushy, I might have already done the deed."

Babe quietly mentioned that the girl had something in her right boot and rambled the possibilities, ending with a weapon.

Trinity woke to the sound of gurgles and coos coming from the nursery. "Girl, Daddy's not home; you'll have to settle for me. After their morning ritual of changing, bath time, and sprucing up for the day, Trinity took the ride down with Chancée. She was sure enough for herself with her legs, but not when hauling the baby up and down the stairs. The baby wasn't as tiny and petite as Trinity, but she wasn't overly big, like Babe.

Ruthie had errands to run, but Trinity elected to stay home. She thought about how things had changed—never a homebody before, but here she was, enjoying being home and not ratting the streets. She curled in a ball on the sofa with Chancée cuddled beside her. "NCIS or Law and Order, and then we'll watch Bluey. Okay?" The baby's bright blue eyes drilled into her as though she knew what her mom had said. An ad for a health club showed a couple working out together, all smiles and laughter. "I call bullshit on that. Nobody is that giddy over sweating their ass off."

Chancée pointed at the screen, "Da-da, Da-da," with a huge smile. Trinity couldn't help but think the baby already had his number. She texted Babe.

Trinity: Your girl watched an ad for a gym with some guy lifting and said Da-da. You been bringing her into the garage?

Babe: Sweet. She's starting to say words. She'll likely be more like you than me and be chatty. I can only hope.

The doorbell rang, which was startling. Trinity got to the door and could see a man trying to look through the beveled glass. She didn't want to seem afraid or nervous but quickly texted Babe about the man at the door. He responded with a quick ignore the door, but she had already started to open the door and inquired, "Yes?" The smell of alcohol was pungent. The man put his foot on the threshold. He looked like a scruffy version of Chris. To calm the air and herself, she quickly commented, "You must be CJ. Chris has told me so much about you. What can I do for you? Please come in. Chris isn't home, but I'll text him and let him know you're here. I know he'll want to see you." The only other person in the house was Jacob, who didn't give much comfort. The guy spooked her. She heard the boy coming down the stairs.

"You got something to eat?" Trinity knew that CJ was working for Glenn, or at least it was the last she heard, although he didn't have the look. He resembled someone living hard on the streets with ground in dirt and smelling of body odor.

Trinity said she'd fix something for him. She didn't want him on the couch; he smelled foul, maybe one of the hard-backed chairs in the dining room. Wherever Jacob went after descending the stairs was anybody's guess. Gunner was missing as well. Of all the times for Ruthie not to be at the house.

She quickly put a sandwich and some chips together with a Coke but could hear him walking around the dining room, probably looking for something to steal. She rushed the food to him. "You got a beer?"

Going back into the kitchen, she texted Chris, informing him of his dad's presence.

> Chris: What?! Get him the fuck out of there. Back on drugs and dangerous. On my way.

She raced back into the dining room with his beer; he sounded more agitated.

"Where's that big husband of yours?" Trinity didn't want to say he wasn't there, but she wasn't good at lying.

She laughed, "Oh, somewhere around here. Not sure." CJ wasn't buying it for one second. "How's the sandwich?"

He stared blankly at her. "No, you wanna know why I'm here."

The service entrance to the dining room slightly and silently cracked open. Jake had the muzzle on Gunner with a tightly held leash. What she didn't see was Babe's handgun in his other hand. Jake crept silently, then said, "Motherfucker, you need to move on down the road, or I'll unleash the dog, and if that doesn't get you movin' out the door, then I'll put a round in your skull." The boy's hand showed no signs of nervousness. His hand was still and completely composed like he'd done it before.

CJ started to turn.

"Uh, uh, uh, just stand and walk your merry ass to the door and get the fuck out of here."

"Boy, you don't have it in you to fire that weapon." Jake pulled the trigger and put one in the guy's thigh. Chris had told him that his dad had returned to his old ways, and he feared he'd pull something like a break-in. As CJ began to turn, Chris came running into the dining room. Jake was ready to fire another shot.

"What are you doing here? I told you to leave me alone. Babe gave you a chance at starting over, and you fucked it up. Chris released Gunner's muzzle and leash. Within a split second, the dog had CJ on the floor with his mouth on the man's throat. "Don't fight him, or he'll fuck you up bad." Jake still had the gun in his hand. Chris looked at him, "You shot my dad?"

"Yes, and the next shot will count if he doesn't leave our house." Trinity sat with eyes wide open and in disbelief at what was happening. The back door opened. Babe rounded the corner with a look nobody had seen; he was scary and intense, his eyes hooded by heavy brows. He walked over to Jake, took the gun out of his hand, and commanded Gunner to his side. The dog responded immediately.

"You." He pointed at CJ, "Follow me. The rest of y'all go 'bout your business. I got it from here."

Max scratched his head. "Trey, what am I gonna do with this chick? You saw her; she's nuts. We know almost for sure she's the serial maniac. We don't have nothing to get a warrant to search her place. Her Grannie might consent, but what if she doesn't? Then, Gwen will know we are onto her and disappear."

Trey reviewed the plan again to get a room at the Hotel Noelle and set it up with audio and video. The connecting room would have monitors and a couple of officers if needed. He'd be perfectly safe. A judge would sign off on everything they did, and it would hold up in court. They'd get the plans set in motion.

Kitty sported a hot pink shoulder-length wig with a pink western hat trimmed in feathers and bling. She wore a hot pink bra under a black fishnet tank and a silver sequined skirt almost up to her ass. Her over-the-knee hot pink boots had four-inch stiletto heels. She looked hot and garnered attention, all outside her standard requests. Three college boys wanted her at the same time. *Nope.* A thirty-something handsome man approached her. His proposition was two hours with his wife while he watched. "That's gonna cost you more." The man didn't care; money wasn't an issue; it was what his wife wanted. She reluctantly agreed. Two hours later, she was back at her favorite location. The next john wanted her for the rest of the night. It would be a most profitable night and quench all his and her desires.

"So Kitty, what's your real name?" he asked. She answered that was her real name. He didn't buy it but went along anyway. "My name is Dwayne." A lump developed in her throat. Flashes of that horrible night with her boyfriend in Memphis ended up being her first murder. It was honestly self-defense, but it started her obsession. This Dwayne had the most enormous, fanciest suite at the hotel. It had a private key for the elevator to the lavish presidential suite.

Dwayne had a mountain of cocaine on a coffee table and bottles of champagne with notes attached. He was a celebrity she'd never heard of or seen before—a rock star. He got his money's worth but wanted her to stay, saying that was the arrangement. The drugs and drinking wasted him into oblivion. A distinct ding sounded, and the private elevator opened with another handsome man. He looked at her, shrugged, and entered one of the bedrooms. She could hear his water running. It was now or never. "Dwayne, Dwayne baby," she shook him. He had passed out. She'd have to work fast and get out of there. She slid the knife from her right boot and slashed away, quickly cleaning behind herself. She pulled the hat low, ensuring she'd hidden her face. She took the elevator down and left the hotel as would be expected.

The headlines on every news channel the following morning would be about the dead celebrity. The story would show her entering with the man called Dwayne. All video clips would feature them laughing and playing, having a good time, nothing violent, and not one shot of her face. The next person in the elevator was the second man. He didn't look happy; in fact, he was more like pissed. They'd slam him as the enraged, jealous lover. She was just the fun call girl that left him with happy endings.

Trey made all the arrangements at Hotel Noelle, and then it was Max' turn to set the date. Antoine Junior was happy to supply whatever the police needed, which cleared the first hurdle. He wondered how fast the sting would get to Trinity and thus Babe.

Max called. She answered. "Gwen, hey, it's me. I'm sorry I've been a downer. Ya know, once bitten twice shy kind of thing. I hope you'll have a private dinner with me at Hotel Noelle and we can spend the night together. Are you interested?" He put on the sweetest, most humble voice he could muster. "Does that undo all my numb-nut blunders? Can we make up?"

Listening to him was nauseating. Trey pantomimed, throwing up, stabbing himself in the heart, and rubbing his eyes like he was crying. Max held up his middle finger but didn't let it interfere with his mission.

Gwen was hesitant at first but then asked where, the time, and was he sure about Hotel Noelle; it was expensive. He said he owed her that for being such a douche. She finally agreed, and they set a date for Friday night; she'd arrive at the hotel at about eight. Since it was Wednesday, it gave him time to plan every detail and hype his nerves.

He'd never been a smooth operator before, which was way out of his wheelhouse.

Trey rocked back in his chair and asked, "You mean to tell me you never tried to be a slick dick and create a romantic interlude for that special someone hoping for some horizontal interaction? Padna, you got it in you; I know you do; you're just a more primal being. It'll be fine. Trust me."

Max began thinking of the things he'd need to bring so it looked authentic—a suitcase with clothes hanging out, as though he'd already settled in, travel toiletries out for display in the bathroom, and a small arrangement of flowers to put on the table. Tech hid mics and cameras in all the most effective places. They ran audio and visual tests out the wazoo. Max and Trey would set the stage, adorning the table with a sampling of appetizers to share. They planned for room service to arrive at eight-thirty with a fancy surf and turf. Slyly, he would comment she was the perfect dessert, but upon Trey's advice, he included chocolate-covered strawberries as a wooing touch.

It was go-time. Max was in room three-twelve. The AV tech, his captain, Trey, and another officer were next door in room three-fourteen. As a precaution, they had a key to Max' room in case she decided to check the doors to the connecting room. Max called her, "You on da way? Come to room three-twelve. Girl, I got a night planned for us and you are the main attraction. Okay, baby, see you soon." Trey and the captain glanced at each other, but there was something unspoken behind the captain's eyes, which caused a slight niggle in Trey's belly. Something felt off, and suddenly, Trey wasn't so sure about the situation. *Too late now.* He turned his attention to Max, who was acting like a high school kid about to get laid for the first time.

Twenty minutes passed, and there were two knocks on the door. Max opened the door with a big smile. "You look great, Gwen." She pushed him hard against the wall and started kissing him. Trey kept an eye on Max but was also aware of the captain's body signals. "Whoa, you knocked me off my feet. Can I take your bag?" She said no and looked at the table.

"Flowers? So sweet. The food looks tasty, but you look tastier." She ran her tongue across her teeth.

"You have to say, she heats it up; Gwen's a hot little number," Big Jim commented off the cuff, maybe unaware that he had said anything aloud. *Say what?* Trey thought.

Max stood behind one of the chairs, directing her to sit. "Before the food gets old. Not as fresh." She sat. He hurried around the table, and the two shared Oysters Bienville, Shrimp Remoulade, and Crabmeat Capris. Another knock on the door. She became fidgety. "Dawlin, that's the guy with our real dinner. Those," pointing at the almost empty tray, "were a tease. They say oysters put lead in the pencil." He double-raised his eyebrows. The man rolled the cart in with silver domed plates, drawn butter, and steak sauces. He presented the dinner by lifting the silver dome—lobster tails and steak. Her eyes twinkled. "I told you I wanted to make up. Looking at you makes me ravenous." *Ravenous*, Trey thought with amusement, probably more to do with nerves. They ate punctuated by small inconsequential talk.

Trey noted that the Captain took an exceptional interest in the case. Maybe it was because they were both from Memphis and they hadn't caught her, but there was an underlying current he couldn't put a finger on. His body movements were animated like he was the one in the room with the psycho bitch. Every time he'd spoken of her, once finding out the name, he'd use her name like one would an old acquaintance. The whole thing had bugged him, not just because of the massacre of men, but usually, the captain would bark out commands wanting them to keep him up to speed, and of course, in front of the news, he'd slyly take the credit. This case was different; the captain seemed more involved, almost on a personal level. Had he known Gwen when she was killing men in Memphis? Was he on the case that went cold? Too many uncomfortable questions.

Max unbuttoned his shirt, signaling to the other room that the action would soon begin. He walked to the bed and drew the sheets back. She flirted, "Has anyone ever handcuffed you to the bed? It makes it more titillating." *Think, think, hell no*, he thought.

He cozied up to her with hands on her shoulders. He whispered, "In my line of work, dawlin, I'm the one with the handcuffs, but I didn't bring them; I'm not thinking 'bout work." She pouted. "Maybe next time," he winked at her.

"I need a quick shower. I want to be fresh for you, especially our first time together. You get undressed while I shower and wait for me in the bed. Now, don't fall asleep." She turned to walk into the bathroom, observing his things strewn on one side of the sink. "I see you left some room for me." She turned on the water. Max started feeling woozy. She'd somehow slipped him a roofie. Shirt off, still with pants on, he slipped under the covers, fighting to stay awake. He whispered, "Roofie," hoping the team in the next room heard him.

He could hear her moving around in the bathroom; the water had stopped running, and she'd be entering any moment. "Ma-a-ax," she seductively sing-songed as she flipped the light switch off and entered the room. "I hope you haven't fallen asleep, you bad boy." She slinked into the room and began moving up his body, knife in hand. The rest of the action was a blur. The team came in; Trey had her in the air; he'd knocked the knife out of her hand. She was screaming and kicking wildly in the air. One of the officers had turned the lights on, and the scene was surreal. She'd managed to nick one of the officer's arms.

Trey snapped the cuffs. "You have the right to remain silent." He continued to Mirandize her as one of the techs wrapped a sheet around her. The captain forcefully grabbed her with a uniform, walking on the other side of her. She stumbled a few times, and the captain would gruffly command her to stay on her feet, always using her name. "Tony," Trey instructed, "grab the clothes she wore here, give 'em to Cap, never mind, give 'em to me. Then, process the shit out of this room." He looked at Max, glassy-eyed, obviously drugged. His body was perfectly still. "You done good. Can you get up and move your arms and legs?" All Max did was grunt, and he slightly moved his appendages, which was not enough to walk out on his own power. Trey radioed for a med team. Max could sleep safely at the hospital and get checked out. "Paramedics are on the way. Be still; tech's gonna scour the room; by that time, your ride will be here. See you later. I'm impressed; you're a natural. I'll pass by the hospital and check on you. Behave." Trey wagged a parental-type finger.

Babe led CJ to the porch. "I could knock the shit out of you. What the fuck were you thinking?" He tore CJ's blood-stained pants. "You're lucky it's a through and through."

After a couple of hours, Babe had his fill of CJ. The phone buzzed, baby in one arm; Trinity picked up the phone with her other hand. "W-Wait. Bethany, slow down. What happened at the hotel?" Trinity intently listened. "Vic," she called loudly. "C'mere. Trey and Max caught the serial killer. Max was dating her?" Trinity put Chancée sitting at her feet and put her free hand to her cheek, mouth gaping in surprise, voice near hysteria. "Oh, my God, what if they hadn't figured it out? How scary is that?"

Babe wanted to know how Bethany knew about the situation. "Is she sure?" he asked Trinity.

"The police department used our hotel. How totally wicked." Babe had his cell phone out to text Trey but then decided against it—the guy was up to his neck in alligators. Trinity turned her attention to CJ on the porch. "What was that all about? He scares me, Babe."

"He should. Girl, he is badass, and combine that with drugs, then there's no conscience; that's a recipe for someone to get hurt. I'm taking him to the V.A. I've warned him not to return here without prior permission. See, I'm not so ludicrous in wanting to keep our home off the radar." She rolled her eyes.

Ten minutes passed after Babe and CJ left when Ruthie came home. Jacob rushed into the kitchen. "We had some shit go down while you were out." *Ker-plunk* he dropped two quarters in the jar. Chris entered the kitchen, and Jacob went silent. Chris told Ruthie about his dad and how Jacob shot him. Ruthie's mouth dropped, and she said she was shocked because he had seemed like a nice fellow. Chris mentioned the drugs; she raised her eyebrows, closed her eyes, and nodded in understanding. Trinity overheard part of the conversation and imagined it would be dinner table talk. First, she wanted the scoop on the serial killer and what happened. Hotel Noelle was getting a reputation for crime and punishment.

With all the ruckus, dinner time was late as was, bath and quiet time—Chris on the phone and Reg and Jake playing games. So much for a peaceful, everyday kind of family. Did they only exist in movies or on the Hallmark channel?

YOU DON'T SAY

The Captain put Gwen in the back of Whittle's unit. As he stretched the seat belt across her, he asked, "What the hell, Gwen? I knew you were hookin' in Memphis, but what's wrong with you killing all those men? Nothin' I can do."

"Jimmy, you said you'd always take care of me." The uniformed officer walked around the unit to the driver's side. "Nobody understands me like you, baby," she whined.

He turned away from her and addressed the officer, "Whittle, bring her to OPP. We caught her in the act; there is no disputing besides it's all recorded." The Captain walked to his car. She knew things about him that would ruin his life. There had to be someone he could negotiate with to silence her.

Gwen went berserk, screaming, "Jimmy, don't leave me. Jimmmy!" She shouted from the deepest part of her soul, "Remember, Big Shot, I got dirt on you, and I'm gonna tell all. Fuck you, Jimmy."

The woman started rambling about the Captain telling Patrolman Whittle things he couldn't unhear. She knew the Captain from when she was a kid. Gwen was fourteen, and he was an adult. She used to talk to him about how her mom's boyfriend was abusing her step-sister. She said she saw it one time when everyone thought she was sleeping. Jimmy had been a strong shoulder to cry on. Finally, one afternoon, while wiping her tears, he kissed her and ran his hand up her blouse. He became her supposed boyfriend and told her he loved her, always had, and would forever.

Finally, he invited her to his apartment, and that's when the heavy sexual interaction began. He wanted to marry her like Elvis had with Priscilla. It was that kind of love, he'd say. He'd brush her hair, rub her back, and make all the bad in her life disappear for the time she had with him.

The day the letter came from the Memphis Police Department was the worst day of her life. He told her it was over and never to speak of their love to anyone and that he would find and marry her when she turned eighteen. As he rose in rank, the promises made to a young girl as he plucked her innocence like a flower disappeared. She found an outlet in the Army until her unquenchable rage provoked a dishonorable discharge, a stain that would never go away.

With venom in her voice, Gwen told Officer Whittle about how Jimmy moved to New Orleans right after she did. Just a coincidence? She warned not to buy that sack of shit's bullshit story.

Back in Memphis, she'd catch him now and then pass by her house. He'd slow down and wave. She'd seen him out a few times; if he were alone, he'd approach her and act like it had been no time at all, but if with his wife and children, he'd only glance her way.

"He's a fucking child abuser. Hey, officer, that the kinda boss you want?"

Patrick Whittle wouldn't even look at her in the rearview mirror. He couldn't get to OPP fast enough, then she'd be their problem.

On more than one occasion, Babe told Trinity about Trey and Max' captain. He'd said he wouldn't be shocked to hear he was corrupt in one way or another. Big Jim threw his weight around, dominating the men and women in his command. Not that Babe was a warm and cuddly kind of guy, but he never thought he was above the Marines he led. He took all the responsibility for them on his shoulders, something their police captain couldn't or wouldn't do.

Trey mulled over the events of the night. It had been perfect. Max pulled it off. The only thing he revealed was his hairy chest. Trey chuckled, remembering Max saying about his big white ass. He felt for the guy. Max finds someone who lights his candle, and she turns out to be a stone-cold killer; at least he got a five-star dinner at Hotel Noelle.

He pulled up to University Hospital, put his official parking pass on the dash, and headed to the E.R. Max was groggy and semi-lucid. "How are you, Padna? I meant it when I said you did a great job. When you whispered Roofie, I barely could hear you and guesstimated that was what you had said. She's one fuckin' nut job, no doubt. Cute girl, great body."

Max nodded with closed eyes. He looked sad from Trey's perspective. "Ain't there no regular chicks in New Orleans that ain't married, gold-diggers, or turned off by the blue?" The guy had liked her a lot at first. "My mind is like a fog. Did I see Big Jim there?" Trey said he did. "What the fuck he's doin' comin' on our case? He ever done you or anyone dat? Somethin's up, I say. My car is at the hotel, you take me to get it?"

Trey felt a pulling in his chest; he knew his partner had strayed far from his comfort zone and turned on his emotional spigot. Life could be unfair at times. Max' dedication to the force brought on the demise of both his marriages. Maybe if he looked at the rank of blue, it'd be a like-minded proposition. A homebody wife couldn't possibly understand the job and might feel alone and dejected. The two girls weren't bitches, cheaters, or possessive, just lonely. The nurse listed instructions in front of Trey and they were clear—no car for at least twelve, if not twenty-four hours, and he was there until discharged.

A couple of hours passed. Max had counted all the ceiling tiles multiple times, but the silence in his heart was overwhelming. There was a light rap outside his cubicle. "Yeah, I'm awake."

Babe stepped inside the closed-off space. "I ran into your boy, Trey, earlier. Trinity's sister told her about the calamity at the hotel, so I passed by. Ma girl wanted me to check on things at the hotel. Tough night for you, I suspect, but from his description, you killed it; perhaps wrong terminology. Anything I can do for you?" He stood tall with hands on his hips.

"Yeah, sit. You might understand I got all these fucked up emotions." Babe tilted his head, listening, but the furrowed eyebrows showed confusion. "I know she was one fucked up person and took the lives of many people, but she was damaged goods. I don't think all serial killers are bad people. You probably think I'm crazy, but I'm worried about the girl in OPP. It's rough in there. Look, Marine, I am well aware there are evil people and natural-born killers, but I don't think that was the case with her." His eyes glassed over. "You think I'm as nuts as she is."

Babe sat with his elbows on his knees, fingers templed, and then put them on his thighs. "No, Max. I don't think you're crazy. Y'all needed to put her away and off the street, no doubt. I suspect her derangement comes from a source deep in her heart. Somebody hurt her; one could speculate that they killed the sweet girl inside her." Babe hesitated, then asked, "Do you want me to check on her? Would that help with your pain?"

Max declined the offer, but it was a meaningful gesture. Babe said he'd made up his mind; he would visit the woman. Her circumstances had tickled his curiosity, he said with a smile. Max wrung his hands, nodded, and said okay, but it was strictly between them—no Trey or anyone else. Max told him about the sting, the roofie, and the initial kiss. "I'd never been kissed like that before. I gotta stop thinkin' about it, if you know what I mean." Babe chuckled.

Max needed to unload, and before Babe knew it, Max told him his life story. He was very descriptive about his two wives and truly regretted putting them in such a situation. "Not everyone can be married to the blue."

"Nor to the Corps. I get it. Trinity is my first girlfriend, now wife, and she's a hot ball of energy. I get not thinking too much about their seductive ways; it can make things uncomfortable in the jeans." Max laughed at his comment but had a hard time believing she was his first. Babe cleared the confusion, "Girlfriend, first girlfriend. I've fucked my way around the world. I'm not trying to boast, but it was what it was. Never any kissing or romance until Trinity. My first was when I hit my teens; the girl, while dressed to look older, was about my age, maybe a little older. She was a working girl, perhaps a runaway, or who knows? I tried to hide her in my grandfather's home, but that didn't work. He was understanding and found her a place to live, and I think he paid her rent until she got on her feet. I don't know. My Far was a wise man—quick-witted, sharper than a tack."

Max rocked his head from ear to ear, sizing up what the big guy had said. "Sounds like a good man. I know about your dad, and the abuse fuckin' sucks. I don't know what kind of Pops I woulda been. I guess it's just not in the cards for me." He looked around the room; Babe could tell he was starting to feel like a caged animal; it was a look one got on their face—fear but not, anger but not, trapped and out of control. "Trey told me you and the missus were out of the country. Where'd you go? I've never been out of the South and surely not out of the country."

"We visited my grandfather's brother in Norway. The two men couldn't have been more different. Far was first-class all the way, but Bjorn, what a piece of work. It was an experience, but I have no desire to go back. Mays, my brother, wants to go back; he got into the Viking shit. Bjorn was all about that and proud of his ancestry. I can see him as barbaric, but not my brother, Mays."

A text came through for Babe.

Trinity: Where y'at?

Babe: Getting ready to leave Max

Trinity: Out of eggs, FYI

Babe: got it. Be home soon.

After another twenty minutes, Babe left.

Officer Patrick Whittle was more than ready to get the psycho out of his car. If what she said was true, their captain was a piece of shit. Should he dismiss it as the rantings of a crazed killer or let one of the detectives look into the matter? It was a heavy topic to keep inside. He knew pedophilia was a sexual preference and couldn't be changed. It'd be like someone trying to convince him that he didn't like women. Patrick knew she was the serial killer; he'd witnessed the action with Detective Sledge. For all her crimes, the death penalty would be on the table; this was one time he thought life without parole would be a fairer sentence if her accusations were solid.

Once in the custody of OPP and having all the proper documentation in his possession, he returned to the precinct with even more paperwork. He only had his part to do; the detectives had the lion's share of the work ahead.

It was strange that the captain hadn't returned. *I guess the brass gets to go home*, he thought. He knew he wouldn't be the lone ranger as Trey was dutiful and would be returning momentarily.

Head into the computer, the officer was fully engrossed in his task. Trey called across the room, "Good job, Whittle. What a shame you had to have the shit end of the stick and bring her to OPP. What a fucking loonie tune." Whittle rolled away from his computer and walked to Trey. "What's on your mind? It was intense and will probably stick with you for a few days, but try not to let it get under your skin. The important thing is she's off the street."

Whittle nervously swayed from side to side. "It's not that, sir." Trey pressed the situation. "She said, and I don't know if it's true, but she seemed detailed in her facts." The detective said for him to spit it out. "She said when captain," he lowered his voice to almost a whisper, "was in Memphis before becoming a cop that he had a sexual relationship with her, and she was only thirteen or fourteen years old. He was an adult with an apartment that he'd take her to. She said she moved here, and the captain coincidentally moved as well. It's creepy, sir. Like he's stalking her." Trey let out a long sigh and told him he was glad he confided in him. "I'm sure you know pedos can't be cured; it's a sexual preference." Trey disgustedly dropped his head and blew out a breath like he was blowing on a burn, saying he knew. Thoughts ran through Trey's head: investigate the captain? Where would he even start? Maybe talk to his contact, Duke Wallace? What would be the read on the situation?

He didn't want to get Max involved; he was already sideways from the whole duplicity. A bounce off of Steph, his wife, was a sure-fired secret kept.

It seemed like there was always something. While the Gwen issue wasn't his to deal with, he felt connected to Max. The big guy would give it a few days and then go to OPP to see Gwen. Babe stopped, picked up a few things at the grocery, and headed home. The whole time, thoughts of the killer percolated in his brain as though there was a riddle to solve. The police caught her in a sting; she was guilty as sin, but there was a piece missing from the story and if he were a betting man, he'd lay cash on the probability of a catalyst.

The more he thought about her, the more he could relate to a few aspects of her personality or more over perversity. Her propensity was punishment for something that happened earlier in her life. The lure used to capture her prey was a man's want of sex. She fed their over-confidence, but unlike her victims, she got her orgasm from the knife penetrating their chest or the element of surprise.

Babe was happy that he could find fulfillment in Trinity's arms, but he also recognized that his terminations gave him a knee-weakening hurrah that would be hard to explain to anyone else. The sheer fact made him a monster or barbarian. Babe was like a coin with two sides, very different yet still the same coin. At this point in his deliberation, he needed Trinity in a most primal way. With skills equal to working girls, their sexual magnetism created a spiritual experience. He considered the Bible verse about marriage—a man taking his wife from her father's home and the two becoming one flesh. He loved that the Good Book had everything covered: brutal slayings, lies, deception, temptation, love, and descriptive, arousing sex. He was starting to get the idea of God, not all the way, but a far piece from where he had begun.

Babe pulled into Chestnut. From where he stood, he could see the family area and the boys kibitzing; the big guy would miss Chris once college started. However, it wouldn't be as long as the time-away deployments if he joined the military. It might be different for Chris; once Babe joined the Marines, it became his family, and he chose not to return to New Orleans. As much as he loved his grandfather, he always felt like a third wheel. It wasn't because of Far; the man was always warm and welcoming; it was his comfort zone in emotional isolation. His cycle of thought was interrupted by the sound of his wife.

"You gonna stand there all night? The mosquitos are gonna get cha, big man. They are the size of Pterodactyls. Reg said that earlier, and I thought it was funny. I had to look the freakin word up. I kinda knew, but now I for sure know." She started to take a step down; he picked up his pace. The brick steps at night could be challenging for anyone. He wasn't taking any chances. "Since you took so long, we ate without you and boy, was it good." She elbowed him in the ribs. "We did eat, but we saved your plate in the warmer." She accepted his tender kiss.

Babe grabbed the plate from the warmer and ate it at the counter. Ruthie entered the kitchen and started up with forty kinds of hell. He quickly rattled, "I only have a few bites left. Hardly worth setting silver, wouldn't you agree?"

"No, I certainly would not. Don't complain to me when you have digestive issues. Eating standing up will give you gas." Trinity burst into laughter and waved her hand under her nose.

He finished his pulled pork in two bites and washed his plate and fork. All the while, Ruthie shook her head in satisfaction. He kissed the top of her head. "Thank you, ma'am. If I find I have gas, it'll be my fault, and I won't be passing any near you."

Ellen, Judge Cleland's assistant, answered his call. "Ellen, James Campbell here; I need to talk with my friend as soon as possible. I have good news for him, but we must act expeditiously; you'll agree once I tell you the subject. We caught the serial killer, and I'm dang sure the feds will be all over this, so we need to pursue asap." Rattled, she patched Big Jim to Judge Felix Cleland.

The baritone voice picked up the call. "Well done, James; Ellen tells me you arrested the serial killer. I understand the urgency. Feds will be sniffing this like a hound dog to vermin. Where is said Satan Spawn? I've been following the reign of terror."

"OPP holding. I don't have to tell you how important getting her through the system is. Feds should have enough on their plate with all the cartel and gang border crossings now that we got someone strict on crime." The judge agreed just as a knock came on the captain's office door. "Take care, my friend, and I know you'll get this done swiftly." They hung up. "Enter."

Rocking side to side, Officer Whittle had a nervous look and manner. His voice was shaky. "I didn't see you come back, sir. Now that we got the killer at OPP and since my shift is long over, do you have any reason I should stay? I did my report."

The Captain said he could leave and told him what a thorough job he did for being his first big case. To the captain, the sooner he could separate his department from the case, the better. Given this was Gwen's introduction to the penal system, she'd be squealing like a pig about their past. He had to get someone to her before the rumor mill began. All he needed was for the feds to look into his background.

OPP was a nightmare. Gwen felt like a fish out of water. The people she encountered were rough, ignorant, and pushing her through. She'd seen enough crime drama that it was obvious they were moving her on the fast track. Some women were tough and abrasive in the Army, but none were stupid. When these people spoke, she had no idea what they were saying. They processed her, arraigned, remanded, and then the fun began. One of the guards told her to strip and shoved her into the shower. She didn't like the way the woman looked at her and was afraid.

"Hey, you didn't have to push me. I was doing everything you asked." The woman told her she'd do whatever she wanted to her and not to complain because nobody gave a hearty shit. This ring of Hell was real; it was the first time she had thought about what she had put so many families through. It was a thrill at the moment, and rarely did she find the need to revisit her actions, although her exploits showed up in her dreams. While it would have been nightmares for others, for Gwen, the dreams had brought on indescribable sexual pleasure, confirmed by damp panties.

Once in the system, time in OPP moved so slowly that one could assess that the authorities had purposefully broken the clocks, but the second hand still ticked around the face as though in slow motion. She was clueless about the process, except for what she'd seen on crime drama shows, which proved unsettling. The public attorney pled not guilty due to insanity. No one bought the insanity excuse. They hadn't given her a chance to call an attorney. They assumed she needed a public defender. She knew what she did was wrong; why didn't she feel guilty? Sizing it up, Gwen pondered there had to be some psychosis that would give her a chance to get out of prison, maybe end up in a psych ward where she could be rehabilitated and eventually return to society. The mere thought process was enough to identify her insanity. Not once did she consider the courts would sentence her to death.

The guards gave her an orange jumpsuit, particularly heinous with her red hair. Reality started peering into her mind when they walked her to a cell and closed the door with a loud metallic bang. Facing her was a big woman, standing five-ten or eleven. *Hell,* she thought, *maybe she's six foot.*

She had tied-back blonde hair, hazel eyes, and an expressionless face. The woman glared at Gwen. The sound of the cage door closing and all the other doors that had closed behind her started sinking in. She began to cry. The big woman exhaled loudly, "For fuck's sake. You wanna cry? I'll give you something to cry about, bitch. Now, shut up, or you ain't gonna make it, and that's a fact. Don't be gettin' on my nerves, or I'll make sure you don't make it. Baby girl, if you know what's good for you, don't fight the guards; go along with whatever they do to you." That message came out loud and clear; the guards raped at will, and nobody ever did anything about it.

Despite Trinity's objection, Babe had made a promise and intended to see it through. Over and over, she repeated that the lunatic tried to kill Max. No matter how many times he told her that Max asked him to check on her, his words fell on deaf ears.

With a hand on her hip and a set jaw, Trinity pushed, "Babe, you gonna let this woman come between us? I don't ask you very often to do or not do something, but this monster killed how many men? Little girls don't have their daddies; mothers will mourn their sons; she doesn't deserve any pity." She shut the bathroom door and locked it. *That's a first.*

"Trinity, open the door." She growled no. He rolled his eyes, cleared his throat, and asked again, "Please open the door." She unlocked the door. Tears streamed down her face. "Don't cry, ma girl. I'll tell Max I won't go if it's that important to you."

"Good," she bustled down the stairs to the kitchen. There had to be a way around it without lying to either Max or Trinity. Maybe he needed to tell him that he couldn't or bring Trinity to see Max; maybe his plea would pull on her heartstrings.

A couple of days had passed, and things had settled from the arrest of Gwen Peters. Trey knew it was just a matter of time before some other crazy ass person upturned the city, but maybe not. It had been a volatile year with Carlton and Gwen Peters. Patrick Whittle called Trey on his cell, even though they were in the same bullpen.

In a guarded whisper, the young officer began, "Detective Kimble, it's Whittle, sir. I have information I'd like to share with you and only you, but it can't happen here. Where can we meet? It's got to be soon." The quake in the officer's voice spoke volumes; it was something substantial.

The request was odd but intriguing. "You familiar with Louie's?" Trey asked.

"Yes, sir," he affirmed. "After work today, okay?" His voice cracked. Whatever the information was, it scared the young officer. Trey confirmed and hung up.

Max came in with a Burger King bag. He handed Trey a wrapped sandwich and a sleeve of little circular hash browns. "I know you don't eat this shit, but I needed someone to eat with me today. Like, some people go tie one on; I eat shit food and don't wanna eat alone. Enjoy, best you can, the egg, bacon, and cheese croissan'wich." He sat and voraciously tucked into his breakfast. For the brief few weeks he had a love interest, he'd cleaned up his manners and appearance. Still, twenty-five pounds down, if he returned to his unhealthy ways, the poundage would return as fast as it came off.

Trey's phone rang again, "Sorry, sir, It's Whittle again. I saw Detective Sledge come in; you can't tell him anything until we talk, and it would probably be even better if you didn't after we talked." Trey answered ten-four. Now, Whittle had truly piqued his curiosity.

Max' phone rang. "Sledge here." Babe quickly said not to say his name. "I gotcha." Babe asked Max to meet him and Trinity at Louie's for lunch. "Will do," and he hung up.

"Will do what?" Trey asked. "You steppin' out on me?" Trey had a grin across his face like the Cheshire cat.

With a bite of food in his mouth, Max answered, "Nah, repair man. I told him I could break from work for a quick noon appointment, and he better be on time. It's my neighbor's son." He slurped down his Diet Coke. "Have you talked with the Captain?" Max shrugged his shoulders and held his hands open wide, fingers spread. "Okay, so this hillbilly motherfucker don't got the time of day to even say hello to me, and since the Gwen thing, he's been up my ass—complimenting me, like joe-buddy. He's got some kinda shit goin' on."

Time dragged on, but eleven-thirty rolled around, and Max left to meet the repairman. Wink. Wink. Trey called Whittle and asked if he wanted to go somewhere and talk. The young officer couldn't break away; their meeting had to be after work.

Finn scooted around the bar when he saw Trinity. "Girl, look atcha. We miss your face around here, especially the old guys. They tell me I make a good drink but not as good as yours." She hugged him tightly and said she missed him too. "You heard Samantha got fired? If anyone asks, I didn't tell ya. Shep walked in on her giving some guy a—well, and that was all she wrote. I bet she's hustling the streets now. Hell, she had a pretty prosperous business here. Anyway, what can I get y'all?" Babe said skins, and they'd go from there. He brought the order back to the kitchen.

"Babe, why'd you want to come here? Nostalgic for the past?" She tilted her head toward her shoulder with questioning eyes. Shep came from the kitchen asking if she wanted her old job. She laughed and said absolutely not. He hugged her and lifted her off the floor. They started reminiscing about the show she and Finn put together. He said they made money like it was Mardi Gras. Trinity scrolled pictures of Chancée.

A few people walked in, and conversation time was over. Trinity relaxed and talked about how good it was to see them. "Now, ma girl, who is getting nostalgic?" Babe asked. She smiled through a few happy tears and kissed Babe's hand.

Max entered Louie's. It had been a while since he'd been. He didn't recognize any faces except the bartender Finn, who used to be the busboy. Trinity and Babe were sitting at one of the corner tables, her back to the door. Max rounded the table; Trinity glared at Babe with anger. "How you two doing?" He took a seat.

Babe cleared his throat. "Max, I need to talk to you. In our last conversation at the hospital, you asked me to check on Gwen at OPP. Trinity feels strongly against the idea, and I understand. I gave you my word, which I take to heart, but my wife's feelings trump everything."

Max' eyes looked sad; he sighed heavily. "I got it. I understand. Maybe I need to see her myself, ya know? I just wanted to know she was okay. The women in there can be ruthless, and I've heard horror stories about the guards beating and raping the women or pushing for sexual favors. It's like the men's prison where one inmate makes another his bitch. The same goes for the women's side, so I hear. She needs to be in a mental hospital, not prison. Trinity, I understand. I ain't mad, disappointed, yeah, but not mad at choo." He smiled weakly.

Trinity felt guilty; she could see the pain in Max' eyes. He really liked the woman a lot. Why did she have to be right out of the cuckoo's nest? She struggled with an internal debate. What harm would it do? It's not like she was going to try to kill Babe. Max was right; she needed to be in a mental facility, but then she thought of all those families affected by the murders of their loved ones. Her anger mounted, and pity flew out of the window; whatever caused her to go off the tracks wasn't their concern. "Babe, what would come from you seeing her? Would you plan on representing her or getting Mays to? She massacred those men, and it was premeditated. She deserves the death penalty."

Max started to get extremely uncomfortable. "Look, y'all, it was a thought, that's all. Babe, I don't want to cause problems with y'all. I see your wife's point. I feel that something caused her to be like that from her childhood." Babe knew all too well what damage could come from a fucked up childhood.

Knowing her husband's issues were caused by an abusive father, maybe it was worth looking into, Trinity pondered. The thought went against every thread of her being. Babe was off the hook for the time being, and he and Trinity could return to their lives without being encumbered by discussions about Gwen.

A VERY SCARY PLACE

Gwen was scared. Certainly, someone would go over her rights and what they expected of her. Was there a rigid schedule? She had heard of OPP being overcrowded, but it was ridiculous. Many of the docuseries she watched showed inmates with a cell to themselves, but obviously, hers came with the big blonde. Things were going much faster than expected, not that she ever considered herself in prison. She figured there would be an orientation, like the do's and don'ts; was there a list of rules or schedules they needed to follow? The only guidelines were big signs posted on the walls. So far, nothing went like it did in the documentaries or anything she read. From what she gathered hearing the prison officers talk, they were planning to put her in the general population. What happened to intake? Giving time to adjust to the new surroundings? Every movie and documentary portrayed the same thing—a thirty-day time of acclimation.

From a few of the shows she watched, she knew not to look at anyone or ask why they were there. The plan was to keep her head down and avoid eye contact. The slightest look from another inmate sounded an alarm to her. She watched as one woman stabbed another with a makeshift knife. As the woman stabbed the inmate, she growled, "I told you to stop mean muggin' me."

The guards broke it up and brought the injured inmate to the infirmary. Gwen noticed one of the guards looking at her. It was day three, and no one had hassled her so far. She kept her eyes focused at a downward tilt, spoke not a word, and stayed to herself. They returned to their cells after the hoopla. The guards had everything under control. Gwen sat quietly on her cot. "Hey Red, Calvin wuz watchin' you hard. He likes himself redheads. Are you real or fake?"

Gwen swallowed hard. "Real, but I have some grey, which I rinse or did."

"Avoid Calvin if you can; he's got evil in him. He gets his jollies hurting us, 'specially first-timers. You look like a first-time. He likes to fuck ev'ry hole you got and put his mark on you." Gwen didn't want to hear anymore. The first day, her cellmate told her not to talk to her or look at her and to stop crying. She was hard and cold, but then, after the knife incident, she suddenly spoke. Gwen decided to continue keeping to herself. As far as she knew, no one was paying her any attention.

It was the time for the disgusting slop they called dinner. Head down, while unappealing as the food was, Gwen didn't want to see if anyone was looking at her. A deep male voice shouted at her, "What'd you say to me?"

Head still down, she answered, "I didn't say anything."

"Now you're callin' me a liar? I heard you say something."

The woman sitting next to her said, "She didn't say nothin'."

"Then, Hartford, maybe it was you." He grabbed her by the back of her jumpsuit, pulled her from the seat, and shoved her toward the cell block.

Everything felt cold and empty of life in the prison. Some of the women seemed friendly with each other, but there was an unspoken distrust palpable in the atmosphere. Nobody trusted anyone. Betrayal was commonplace; inmates did what they had to to get what they wanted.

A young black girl sat across from Gwen, hair short and braided close to her scalp. Tattoos covered her arms, and she had what looked to be a teardrop tattooed under her eye. As though boring holes, she drilled through Gwen with dead, dull eyes, then put her hand to her mouth and stuck her tongue between two fingers. What was the gesture? She knew what it implied, but who was part of the action was a mystery. Did she want to do Gwen or the opposite? Whatever, nothing was going to happen; Gwen didn't butter her bread that way. The girl huffed out a loud breath as if saying Gwen had no choice; whatever the plan, it was inevitable. Dinner ended, and like cattle, they filed into their cell block.

The herd moved with a hum of quiet conversations with the occasional outburst. In the distance, they could hear a woman, her words unclear, but everyone knew, though ignored, it was Hartford. After manhandling her out of the dining area, the guard had his way with her. Nobody seemed to care. It was like any other evening in OPP.

Walking into her cell, the black girl and two of her group shoved her to the floor. Two women held her down while the girl with the braids stripped off the jumpsuit and forced herself on Gwen with harsh actions that hurt like she wanted to prove a point.

The sound of a low, rumbled, hate-filled growl filled the air. The accost stopped, but she bit Gwen on the thigh as a parting gesture, enough that it bled. Gwen's chest was tight, preventing her lungs from filling. She wanted to scream, vomit, and wail at the same time. Through tears, she quietly mumbled to the big blonde, "Thank you."

"Don't thank me; I don't let others play with my toys. Make no mistake, your scrawny ass is mine, and you'll beg for more. I wanna give it enough time that you are aching for your man."

Gwen, still in a muffled voice, said, "I'm not a lesbian."

With a husky laugh and a heavy helping of sarcasm, she confidently said in a monotone voice, "Give it enough time, and you will be."

Trinity curled in the contours of Babe's body. The space he created on his side provided the perfect place for his tiny woman to cozy next to him. She heard his quiet snores, but maybe it was purrs of dozing or contentment, not sleeping. He did that sometimes. Perhaps it was due to the heavy muscles in his chest. She whispered, "Vic?" He acknowledged by saying hm. "You awake?" She prodded.

"I am now for sure." He drew her closer to him. "Can you feel how awake I am?" He chuckled with a grunt as his body rubbed against hers.

"If you want to talk to the psycho on behalf of Max, I guess it's okay. It's not like she can hurt you; there's bound to be tons of guards." He couldn't hold it in and snickered, implying, 'really?' "I mean it, Vic. They say insane people are twice as strong as regular people."

He rolled over, his body resting on his elbows, hovering over her. "And I'm regular people? If you have no objection, slide your drawers off."

She wiggled, scooting her underwear off. "Um, don't you mean panties? Ladies don't wear drawers, Vic. Now, shush and make love to me."

Trey walked into Louie's. It had been a while since he'd been there. Memories of all the shit that went down in there or memories of the people there brought the past screaming to the forefront of his mind. He missed coming in and seeing the big guy sitting at the end of the bar and the pretty little Creole bartender dancing as she poured excellent drinks. That year had been something else. While things were hardly quiet or serene, the past few years had opened his eyes to the future. He was feeling a bit nostalgic.

"No way," Finn shook his head, "What is it about today; it's like old home week—first Babe and Trinity, and now you. "What ya havin'?"

"Spinach dip and a water with lime. I'm meeting someone from the P.D. here. I'm gonna grab a table in the corner. If you see a uniform come in, point my way, please. Thanks, Finn. By the way, I never told you that I instinctively knew you hadn't been the culprit in that Spring break thing. I'm sorry I harassed you the way I did; I was just doing my job. No hard feelings?"

Finn nodded with a smile, "You were up my ass sideways, scaring the living crap outta me. Damn, you're good at interrogations, dude." Finn dropped the order in the kitchen and made his drink, bringing it to the corner table when a young-looking police officer entered Louie's. Finn waved him over and took his drink order, pointing to Trey.

Whittle placed his order, sat with Trey, and began telling the Gwen story. At first, probably due to nerves, he was all over the place. Trey went into interview mode, getting the young officer to settle. The story was one Max needed to hear. It would explain a lot. Trey had gotten weird vibes about the captain from the get-go. He was a pompous, throw-his-weight-around asshole. He had no respect for the rank and file.

Since the workday was over, Trey ordered a beer. Looking at Whittle's posture and movements, other than being nervous, every word out of his mouth was true. Their superior was a pedophile. Maybe it was just a strong attraction to Gwen; regardless, it was against the law. She was barely in her teens, so the story went. A question popped in his head. He felt confident that Whittle hadn't made up the saga, but had Gwen concocted a lie? Trey's mind spun, trying to figure out different scenarios. Why would she? Memphis was a vast place, and it so happened that she knew the new captain some twenty-five years earlier. She could have tried to smudge Max' name like he had been forceful or violent with her, and that's what drove her to pull a knife on him. It had merely been coincidental that the serial killer used a knife. She could have built a story several different ways—role play could be one. Gwen didn't know about the sting at the time. No, it was what it looked like—the woman was a sick piece of shit and had killed around twenty men, combining Memphis and New Orleans. Period. The Feds would be on the case like white on rice.

Trey had noticed a few Fed-looking people in and out, yet they hadn't staked a claim. There wasn't an investigation; they caught it all electronically. Up to that point, the media wasn't hounding them; it was as though the story had died off. The news did more publicity on a big drug raid. Were they lining up the dominos, or had it something to do with the Memphis unsolved murders? Whatever the case, it was perplexing.

Before Trey could ask Whittle to go back over what Gwen had said to him, the officer started the story again; this time, he was far calmer and remembered more details. The men postulated on the oddity of it all. Such a petite woman to mutilate men. Some of her victims had been well-built and far stronger than her. Had she drugged them all?

Back in OPP, things had gone from bad to worse. Several inmates had raped and roughed her up. Her blonde cellmate beat the crap out of a couple of the women, and the guards brought her to the Hole. She had inflicted massive injury by having a lock tied in a sock, which cost her added time to her sentence. Gwen was on her own to fend for herself.

Mid-morning, one of the guards came to her cell. Going through her mind was *rape, blow job?* Instead of the more undesirable things, they told her she had a visitor. She hadn't told anyone she was in jail; how could she have a visitor? She hadn't put any names on a visitor list. She hadn't made a phone call; there was no one to call. All she had was the Public Defender. He led her to an open room with tables and chairs. The shock took her breath away.

"Hi, Gwen," he smiled at her. It was a genuine smile, not forced, like he was happy to see her. She didn't remember the deep dimples. "How you holdin' up? I know they got some hardcore in here."

She started to speak but stammered, "I-I can't believe you came to see me, Max. You look good." He handed her a stick of gum, and the guard closely observed, even though he knew Max was a cop. "I have no words to say, sorry." She pleadingly looked at him.

"Gwen, there are no words. You are who you are. I don't get it, but it's not mine to get. I like you." Max turned his hand palms up and smiled. "So, you have a fetish? No one's perfect." She smiled back. "Would you tell me your story? I don't need gory details, but how did this all begin?"

She looked down, and a tear fell from her eyes. She sniffled. "We don't have enough time. I'll write you a letter. It'll give me something to focus on." Max handed her his business card and a clean handkerchief from his pocket. "I'd like to touch your hand. But the guard told me no touching." She gazed at him, and like a tidal wave, her mind flooded with snaps of that night. It opened Pandora's box, and images of all the men poured through like a breach in a dam. It was more than she could handle. She choked up and said, "I can't; I gotta go. Thanks for coming." She stood and signaled the guard, who inspected the hankie and made her spit out the gum.

Max watched as she walked away. Gwen didn't look back even once.

After retrieving his things, he noticed a missed call from Trey. "You rang?" Max questioned in a jovial tone.

"Uh, yeah, where you at? I gotta talk to you. Meet at Mother's?"

"Why you do me dat? I'm trimming my physique." Trey laughed out loud. "You dick, I am. I'll meet you. Gimme fifteen minutes with traffic." Trey asked again where he was. "I'll tell ya when I see ya."

Even though it was behind bars and knowing she wanted to kill him, it was good to see Gwen. He wondered if any of her attention was an attraction to him or just setting him up to be her next victim, the ultimate conquest. Was any of it real? All her probing and relentless questions made sense now that he knew who or what she was. His mind rambled. *Boy, do I pick 'em.*

Max pulled up to Mother's; Trey was leaning on his car. He glanced at his watch, "You nailed it, fifteen minutes to the second. Now, where ya been?" He grabbed Max' bicep. "You all secret secret. I know you don't have another fish on the line yet."

The older detective put his hands in his pockets. He knew he'd get a tongue-lashing when he told him. "I went to see Gwen." Silence.

Trey squared off his eyes squinting. He looked off into the traffic going up and down Poydras. "Are you fuckin' nuts? I gotta put a leash back on you. Whatever, Max. Now, I have some interesting info you're not going to believe. I met Patrick Whittle yesterday evening at Louie's."

Max' eyebrows shot up. "No shit, I was there yesterday meeting Babe and Trinity. Anyway, what's this Patrick Whittle gotta say?" Trey ran down the accusations made by Gwen concerning the captain. Max' jaw dropped as the explanation unfolded. "Poor girl. It's no wonder she's fucked in the head. Trey, that means he's a fuckin' pedophile. I wonder who else knows. What about your contact in Memphis? Maybe he got drummed out of there because of suspicions." They got in line. "You bitch me out when I brought you a sandwich, and here you are, making me stray off my healthy habits. Some friend."

Max mentioned Gwen looked roughed up. They talked about brutality rumors they'd heard regarding OPP. Trey was quick to point out, "Feds are on it now. They'll move her for sure to some fed prison." They ate the rest of their lunch in silence, both theorizing different scenarios. "Max, what if the feds are looking into the captain? You know, if he was into teenage girls, I bet he has lotsa kiddie porn on his computer. Feds don't come around unless they got the perve dead to rights. It's just a formality. Maybe it has nothing to do with Gwen." Both shook their head and said nah, that Gwen was going to federal prison and probably was going to get the death sentence or life without parole. With women's movements and demanding equality, death sentences became more prevalent for women. Some waited ten years on death row for their lethal injection with no interaction with other people.

"I'd go fucking nuts," Trey sighed.

"Hey, douche, they are insane." His smile was empty.

Trey pulled out his phone and tapped into a number, holding up his pointer for Max to hold tight. "Duke, this is Trey from New Orleans." Silence for a few moments. Trey pointed to the door, and they left. Max sat in Trey's car. "I'm putting you on speaker; my partner Max is in the car. Yeah, you heard right, we got the serial killer. I want to ask you something, but you gotta keep it close to your vest." Duke agreed and asked him what they needed. "Were there ever any rumors regarding James Campbell? Like any straddling the line of legalities or scruples?"

They heard Duke take a deep breath and exhale with force. "What I got, y'all, is whispers but no fact or evidence. A few of the guys in the department, none here anymore, were big into asking for sexual favors and into porn. Look, I don't care what people do on their own time, but I heard, that's heard," he stressed, "they were watching it in the station. Is that what y'all are talking about because it's old stuff? Our house is clean as a whistle."

The situations were similar and smacked of the same perversion, but doing a kid and watching a kid porn flick were different. "No, but kinda. Anything to do with Gwen Peters?"

"Before my time, y'all, but after being with you and you having a picture of Gwen, I asked some of the oldtimers. They said little Gwen was head over heels for Jimmy before his time on the force. They'd hang out at the ice cream shop, or she'd ride around with him in his car. Some of the guys thought the optics were questionable, but her aunt and uncle never made a complaint, and they complained about everything—dog barking, music too loud, long grass, you got the idea. If there were something sketchy, they'd have called it in. Shit, Jimmy was eight years older than Gwen, if not more. The guys told me that as soon as Jimmy joined the blue line, the sightings of Jimmy with the girl vanished."

The New Orleans duo listened with perked ears. "Once again, close to the vest, Gwen Peters is the killer. We have solid proof, beyond any shadow of a doubt, and that's for another conversation. The officer that brought her to OPP, Orleans Parish Prison, said she railed on about how Jimmy took her to his apartment when she was thirteen or fourteen for sex but dropped her like a lead balloon when the Memphis P.D. accepted him, academy, yada, yada. He promised the kid that he would marry her as soon as she turned eighteen— a bit like the check's in the mail, and I won't cum in your mouth. The girl was heartbroken and apparently still is after all these years."

"Gotcha." Thanks for the 411.

"She's awaiting trial, and it'll be a long wait. The courts have trials out the yin-yang probably enough for the next several years. I don't know; maybe because of how horrible the crimes are, they'll move it faster, and then she'll be off to federal prison. I'm surprised there hasn't been more national news about the whole thing. Somebody is controlling what gets into the media. She killed near twenty men; it gets ya thinkin', who's holding the reins? Thanks, Duke."

"Yeah, Duke, thanks; this is Max Sledge, Trey's better half," they both had a chuckle.

"Anytime, boys."

Max and Trey sat quietly, both wrapped in thought. Trey broke the silence and took Max to task for going to see Gwen. "I bet she was surprised to see your ass. Who in their right mind still pines for someone who planned to execute them? Man, get one of the working girls and have them suck the crazy out of you. Cherie used to be your special one, right?"

DIRTY BLUE LINE

*M*id-rep with the heavyweights, Babe's phone buzzed. He dropped the weights on the rubber-matted floor. It was Trey. He thought, *what scuttlebutt do they have now?* Reluctantly, he answered. "Vicarelli, what ya got, Trey?"

"Feds are all over the Gwen case, and I can tell they're trying to put some pieces together. Remember the Spring breakers?" Babe rolled his eyes; of course, he remembered. I want to do something like that with the Captain. Not his office or car. If I could hear him talk about Gwen or—"

Babe told him to give it a rest. He understood he didn't like dirty cops or ones with a penchant for young girls, but he couldn't be with the Captain twenty-four-seven. The big guy said he'd mull it over and get back to him if he had anything worth offering. He rushed the detective off of the call, resuming his routine. He powered through most of it when Trinity entered. "Did you forget that today is moving day for Chris? He has his Bronco stuffed. I can't believe the amount of shit he has accumulated and thinks necessary to bring to the dorm."

He cocked his head to the right, then reminded her who bought all the shit for the dorm. She stopped talking momentarily and then told him to finish his workout, as it might adjust his attitude. "My attitude?" *Are you fuckin' kidding me?* She had cahonas the size of bowling balls for such a tiny thing. How so much attitude fit in –" his mind drifted, and he called Trey back.

"It's Babe. Does your cap have the new high-tech watch that links with his phone? If so, you can listen; it might sound garbled if his phone is in a pocket. Somebody needs to talk to the Feds; they have all the newest toys. Are they in the house yet?"

Trey was excited; he thought Babe's idea was solid. Big Jim often would brag about his high-tech watch to the pions below him. The thing was, most of the younger cops had the same thing. If the Feds played ball with the P.D., they would have the equipment to record his conversations. Getting them to buy into the story was another hurdle. As a rule, they looked down on local leos. Trey said he'd seen a couple come in and out, but they didn't talk to him, only their Captain.

Babe knew two people who might have connections to the FBI for an intro. One would be clean and the other a dirty agent. Calling Coach for a favor seemed inappropriate with all he was going through. The coach had made it abundantly clear when Babe and Trinity had him and his wife to dinner that he didn't want a pity party and emphatically said it would be the last time Babe would see him. Not that it was his preference, but he called Javier.

The line buzzed a few times. "And what do I owe for this pleasure, Marine? How has life as a civilian been treating you since we last met? It is peaceful here, which is a glaring contrast to Cartagena." His English was too precise and didn't flow naturally, but it was better than Babe's extremely limited Spanish vocabulary.

The two friends talked for a half hour, catching up and teasing each other.

"Javi, you sound lonely. I know I miss aspects of my past with a longing. Civilian life doesn't suit my personality; there's too much laying back or empty time. My friend, do you have any connections with the FBI? We got a dirty head-honcho cop, and I find him annoying. You won't be bothered by his actions, but I am. It's a moral thing."

The air went silent, but he could hear Javi breathing. Finally, he spoke, "A moral thing? Like I have no morals? Funny you are asking for a favor, yet slay me with condemnation. He crossed a line: do what you do, Marine, or have you lost your touch?" Silence filled the air again. "You want him taken down on the carpet, is that it? Then, I say, that's ego and control not taking care of business. What do you say to that?"

Babe cleared his throat, "Probably. Thanks for the boot up my ass. I'm way too civilian, my friend. Like I have a heavy conscience, having emotions suck. Sometimes, I think I preferred numb." Javi had been right; rather than go through espionage bullshit and too many people involved, he needed to take care of the issue. Like Trinity once said to him, keep it simple, stupid. They ended the conversation; Babe agreed that he and Trinity would visit him in Barcelona.

Babe rocked back in his chair, putting his feet on the desk. It would have to be quick and absolute. Trey and Max had said their boss kept banker's hours. That would make stealth difficult. What about his health club? He'd need to do some reconnaissance.

Telling his detective pals that he'd made some connections that might stay them for a while. He'd only reveal an anonymous person would deliver the information on their dirty cop to the feds. They could get back to work and leave thoughts and plans for the Captain. It was gonna be a done deal.

Babe tailed the Captain steady for two weeks. He had a predictable routine until one evening when he left work at five; instead of going to the health club, he went to OPP. How audacious could the man be? He fucked up Gwen's adolescence, used her until he didn't need her anymore, and now Big Jim was going to rekindle the pain. She was behind bars with no life, and he could walk out easy as you please and fuck somebody else up.

OPP was in a rough area with poor street lighting. Maybe he could strike before the piece of shit had a chance to fuck with her head. He'd ask Trey or Max to talk to the powers that be and add him to her visitor list. He could then confirm, face to face, that Captain James Campbell, James, Big Jim, or Jimmy was gone for good.

The Captain parked his car and sat in it for at least half an hour, then started it up again and took off. Maybe he felt shameful, which he damn well should, or he had another plan up his sleeve. Babe followed him to a bar on Canal Street, almost to the cemeteries. He hadn't been in the bar for more than fifteen minutes when he walked out, beer in hand, with a scuzzy-looking person. It reminded him of Chop, probably strung out on drugs. Was this who the high and mighty Captain James Campbell associated with? No way. After handing the man a manilla envelope, the man walked to a beat-up Mercury Marquis.

Babe followed the Chop look-alike. He knew he could get the information out of him. He turned down a street off Orleans and pulled up to a fourplex made from one house. A crowd of people, probably ten, hung out on the porch. They called out to the scrawny, junked-out man, obviously from a similar flock. *Birds of a feather, yada yada.* Babe scratched the address on a piece of paper and pulled behind a vehicle parked on the side of the road. He walked down a couple of houses and stopped at the gathering.

He climbed the first few steps. "Excuse me, does a Vincent St. Germain live here? This is the address he gave me. He held the paper out. A flirtatious girl stepped down and took the paper from his hand.

"Dawlin' you got the right address, but ain't no one named Vincent here. We got a Vince, but he got a normal last name." She was high as a kite. "You want to party with us?" She batted her eyes. He was pretty sure he could get an STD just standing next to her. One of the guys yelled at her to stop bothering the big guy and to get her ass upstairs. The skinny guy with the manilla envelope stepped from the porch and started down the steps, puffing his chest out. *You've got to be kidding me*, Babe thought.

"Back on outta here, brother, or you might find yourself in a hot mess." He chuckled, looking back at the group. One flashed a piece. Scuzz-bucket raised his eyebrows and pursed his lips. "See ya, wouldn't wanna be ya."

In a low voice, Babe turned to walk away and said, "I seen ya take the money from Jimmy." He kept on walking.

The guy ran up to him. "W-wait. You know Jimmy?"

"Fuck, yeah, who don't? I done a few things for him." Babe wanted to sound authentic to mix in with the type of people hanging around. The guy started babbling non-stop. He explained the money wasn't for him, but he was saving it for his sister, who was in OPP. Something might happen to someone," he winked, "if ya get my meanin', so the money's hers for when she gets out."

"I gotcha, bro. I thought Vincent St. Germain was the one, never mind—" Babe implied that the person he sought was involved in the same deed.

Jiggling like a Hawaiian figure on the dash of a car, the guy introduced himself as J.J. and said that the job was a one-pony circus. Babe nodded and continued to his truck. *So, he's put out a hit.* He slid into his vehicle and took off. He punched in his recent calls. An aggravated voice answered, "Marine, do you know what time it is here? You have me now, so what's the emergency?"

"I need you to move Gwen Peters from OPP to a federal prison. The captain of the police precinct just put out a hit on the girl. She's bad news, but the story is long. Let's just say she has a way with knives and men."

"The serial killer? It's been on our news. They say she killed twenty men as part of a sexual ritual. That is one sick fuck. I'm surprised she hasn't already gone to federal prison. That, my big friend, I can do. You do know she is going to die anyway? Lethal injection, and there is nothing anyone can do about it, not even you."

The path for Gwen Peters was a one-way street; she deserved it, and as far as he was concerned, he'd take lethal injection over life without parole every damn day, but that was how he felt. Maybe Gwen felt different about it. She needed psychiatric help, but one could easily say that of most of the inmates. What she did was sick and hideous and only satisfied one person. It was a game to her, whereas he took trash off the streets, making New Orleans a safer place.

Whether it was Max or Trey, one of them managed to get Babe

on Gwen's visitor list. She might be better prepared if he could give her a heads-up. He didn't want to tell the detectives about the hit or rushed transfer; they'd ask how he knew. He had already said too many times that he wasn't a kiss-and-tell kind of guy or his mysterious superpower, always tongue-in-cheek. He always had a comeback that ended the conversation. They had laughed it off, but Babe knew his repartees were wearing thin. Deep in his soul, there was a yearning to call it quits. Gino was supposed to be the last extermination, but that plan went quickly by the wayside. Why did Trinity's, and yes, now his Loving God, allow such atrocities?

Trinity was in a funk. She wasn't her usual b-boppin' self. It amazed him how her emotions transferred to him, and he could feel the hurt. "What's up, my sexy lady?" Babe asked, hugging her from behind. He blew on her neck, making her giggle, but something was awry.

"I miss Chris, Babe. Can we see him and bring Reg to see Stuart? We'll have to call Stuart first. Of course, we'd take Jake; I know he misses him like mad. The three act like brothers. I know they argue and complain, but it's just like my brothers when they were younger." Chris had been good to Reg and brought him to see his godfather a few times, and Stuart had come to the house to visit Reg. They were developing a strong bond, which hit Trinity and Babe in the feels.

Babe hugged her tight and agreed. With the whole Captain, Gwen thing, the big guy had been absent, maybe making her feel more lonely for Chris, making his heart swell and stifling his breath. No doubt, their souls were connected.

After a quick call to Stuart, Trinity sealed the plans, and they would be heading to see Chris the following morning. Babe pondered to himself; nothing ever came from Elloise's death. Reg, Stuart, or Austin didn't speak of her; it was as though she never existed. *Just as well*, he thought.

Sharing time with Chris filled her void, and Trinity went back to her feisty, playful self. Babe made a mental note that they'd have to do that more often.

Playing wannabe cop, Babe could easily be distracted from their home life. It was obvious he was looking for a purpose. Trinity had suggested opening up a New Orleans branch of Mays' law firm, becoming an investigator for insurance claims, or even opening a studio where he could teach self-defense. None of it was appealing. She'd noticed he was taking longer runs, obsessed with having sex, but it wasn't the passion; it was filling time. Even Ruthie had mentioned the difference. The man was empty without a purpose. Having wealth was handy, but it didn't ground him. Trinity said maybe pray about it. *Yeah, I'll do that,* he sarcastically thought.

Then it happened: Babe's cell buzzed, and instantly, his face wasn't as tense as if his demeanor had changed; it was like the man was back to himself. Trinity had to ask who had been on the phone, thinking about who or what could have made such an impact.

A big, crooked smile crossed Babe's face, and the twinkle returned to his eyes. He answered, "Jarvis."

COMPLEXITIES: OTHERWISE KNOWN AS FOOD FOR THOUGHT

Babe's mission with Jarvis not only gave him Jacob but he had a good look at the atrocities of human trafficking. He wanted to make a difference, and as much as Javier said, it was pointless—What if God had heard their prayers? Maybe the United States would cast away all the corruption and pay off money to enemy countries. Just what if? Remember how Jarvis' mission brought a new quest for Babe?

There was still the problem with the pedophile, Captain "Big Jim," and Gwen's transfer to federal prison. There was always something around the next turn, but if he could use his tactical skills for a warrior like Jarvis, he could find purpose. The missions might only be once or twice a year, but that would be enough to satisfy his needs while doing something honorable. It was his to do.

The questions to consider:

Does anything transpire with Trey and Max regarding their new captain?

Does "Big Jim" get his comeuppance?

What was the mission with Jarvis? Was it the same as before or a new crisis?

Is there someone in the background who penetrates Babe's secrets?

Discover answers to these questions in the seventh book in the FIT THE CRIME series, *The I Lie. Visit my website:* corinnearrowood.com, for the latest scoop!

As always, I wish you love,   Corinne

MANY THANKS

The more my writing progresses, the longer my list of acknowledgments becomes—so many wonderful people along the journey. I feel truly blessed.

I will always thank Doug, my handsome and loving husband of almost thirty-eight years. He is the love of my life, cream in my coffee, butter on my bread, as I am his. We're both like kids, just with many years of experience. Have I ever mentioned he is smashingly good-looking and ten years my junior? I was a Cougar before there were Cougars! *Thank you, God.* The bulls**t he puts up with me and my incessant questions is, I'm sure, taxing, but he never complains; he only says, "Wait, who did what?" Thank you for patiently waiting while I finish one more thought, which turns into a chapter hours later. Your support and encouragement give me the boost to continue my passion.

Thank you to our adult children and their husbands and wives for cheering me on, attending my release events, and inviting your friends. While I've known or met most of your friends throughout the years, having them as my readers brings us closer together, and I love it. The more, the merrier makes for a great party.

Thank you to our talented grandchildren, each making a mark on the world. Thank you for sharing that your Nana is an author.

Continued thanks to the Lunch Bunch. Bobbie, Kaki, Betsy, Susie, Kit, and the occasional surprise of Mary Catherine, y'all have been onboard with me since the first book. Great lunches, lots of laughs, and heartfelt conversation—Thank you, ladies, for your friendship and willingness to hear my constant chatter about new storylines. I love our Wednesday lunches, and one day, I will write *Tales of Time and Wisdom* delivered by the Lunch Bunch.

Thank you, Paige Brannon Gunter, for being the editor I need. Each time I finish a manuscript, I ask if you'll still take time for my book. It makes me nervous. What if she says she's too busy or it's not her thing anymore? You've taught me more than you know. I can always count on your honest opinions and suggestions. You help me keep continuity in my books, catch the uh-ohs, and respond when I need a jump start. I love that you love the characters and appreciate their growth. Hopefully, you will be my forever editor. Have no fear; I will be your forever fan. Congrats on starting your book. Woo Hoo!

Thank you, Kaye Chetta, for your rah-rah support and for being the second reader in the stable. Your support is invaluable. I look forward to more reading adventures together.

Thank you to Kristen Collura, who gathers friends from all over to my book signings and events.

Words cannot express my appreciation to Cyrus Wraith Walker. A fun fact—he's the one that found Captain Babe Vicarelli so that y'all can put a face (and body, yes, indeed!) to the name. He understands what I want as a cover design even when I can't describe it. You are absolutely amazing and bubbling over with talent. You are the real deal! Thank you for creating each book as a work of art. Our study has all my cover designs as artwork. Everyone loves our study!

I cannot express my appreciation enough to the readers who have followed my journey. I strive to quench your desire for adventure and relationships with my characters. I hope you enjoyed *The Impenetrable Lie*.

I offer my utmost gratitude to the men and women of the Armed Forces for their dedication, courage, and resolve to protect our country. It is with heartfelt thanks to the families and friends of our brave men and women of the Armed Forces, who sacrifice so much. Our prayers are with you and your loved ones. One of our grandsons, Brennon McWhorter, is in the Navy and has been deployed. Thank you, Bren, for your service and Godspeed. May He keep you safe in your journey.

The statistics of PTSD are staggering. Many of our Marines, soldiers, and sailors come home entrenched in the horrors they experienced and the nightmares they cannot escape. If you know one of our heroes who might be suffering from PTSD, contact the Wounded Warrior Project, National Center for PTSD, VA Caregiver Support Line at 888-823-7458.

Statistics show there are between 13 and 15 veteran suicides every day. Pray for our men and women of the Armed Forces and support them as they return home. Get help from the Veterans Crisis Line. Call 988 (Press 1) or text 838255.

OTHER BOOKS BY THE AUTHOR

Censored Time Trilogy
A Quarter Past Love (Book I)
Half Past Hate (Book II)
A Strike Past Time (Book III)

Friends Always
A Seat at the Table
PRICE TO PAY
The Presence Between

Fit the Crime Series
The Innocence Lie (Book I)
The Identity Lie (Book II)
The Impossible Lie (Book III)
The Inevitable Lie (Book IV)
The Impostor Lie (Book V)
The Impenetrable Lie (Book VI)

Be On the Look Out for…
The I Lie (Book VII of the Fit The Crime series.)

Visit my website, corinnearrowood.com, and register to win freebies
Reviews are appreciated

ABOUT THE AUTHOR

According to Me:

Local girl to the core. There's nowhere on earth like New Orleans! I am still very much in love with my husband of over thirty-eight years, handsome hunk, Doug. I'm a Mom, Nana, and great-Nana. (four kids, thirteen grands, three great-grands) Favorite activities include hanging with the hubs, watching grandkids' games and activities, hiking, reading, and traveling. I am addicted to watching The Premier League, particularly Liverpool—The real football—married to a Brit; what can I say? I'm living my best life writing and playing with my characters and their stories. I'm a Girl Raised In The South (G.R.I.T.S.) Perhaps the most important thing about me is my faith in God. All of my characters, thus far, have opened a closed heart to an open one filled with Light. Some take longer than others.

According to the Editors:

Born and raised in the enchanting city of New Orleans, the author lends a flavor of authenticity to her books and the characters that come to life in stories of love, lust, betrayal, and murder. Her vivid style of storytelling transports the reader to the very streets of New Orleans with its unique sights, smells, and intoxicating culture.

www.ingramcontent.com/pod-product-compliance
Lightning Source LLC
Chambersburg PA
CBHW031049310726

48969CB00007B/2188